SPIKE & MALICE

MALICE

MAGICKAL MULE MYSTERY BOOK TWO

JEN KENNING

Publishing Coordinator – Sharon Kizziah-Holmes

Paperback-Press
an imprint Paperback Press, LLC
Springfield, Missouri

ISBN - 978-1-964559-63-6

DEDICATION

I am so very grateful for the many people in my life, both living and passed. Their encouragement, lessons, love, and guidance have been the keys to my being able to put words on a page.

ACKNOWLEDGMENTS

Special thanks to fellow author, Susan Keene, for editing this book and encouraging me to keep writing.

Thanks to Janet Kay Gallagher for her proofreading expertise.

I'm grateful to Sharon Kizziah-Holmes of Paperback Press for publishing me and for the beautiful formatting of my manuscripts.

Jaycee DeLorenzo did a great job on the cover, I couldn't stump her with a request for an antique, steam powered tractor with a bale spike.

CHAPTER 1

What in the world is all that noise? I started to roll over and reach for my phone to check the time. The weight on my left arm made it difficult to move. Isabella, my very round calico cat, was sprawled across my arm and dug her claws in when I pulled my arm from under her tummy. "Ow! Issy, let me up."

I flailed out of bed and hurried out the bedroom door and down the hallway. I pulled my robe on as I went. The cacophony of need was much louder and more urgent than most mornings, not to mention about two hours earlier than normal. Sophia, my 10-pound fluffy mutt was losing her mind at the back door. She barked, growled and scratched at the door as if she could dig through it. She was accompanied by Violet, a Chihuahua, who had been our houseguest for a while.

"Hush, dogs, y'all are going to wake the entire house." *And possibly some dead folks too.* I reached for the doorknob to let the mutts out and thought better of it. *What if there is a skunk out there? Or worse?*

"Fen, what in the wide world is going on out here?" Lester asked.

1

I jumped. "Ahhh, dang it, you scared me, Lester."

"I'm sorry about that, didn't mean to. Violet tore out of bed like her feet were on fire and her tail was catching. The way her and Sophie were barking I figured I better see if we were under attack," Lester said.

"I don't know what has them so worked up. I was thinking of letting them out, but it could be something awful, a skunk or something that can hurt a couple small dogs. How about we put them in the laundry room for a few minutes and I'll go out and look around with a flashlight."

"Good idea, except you're not going alone. Fenreya Stern, do not argue with your elder. I know this is your house and I am your houseguest, but I am also a grown man, and your father would flip in his grave and haunt me if I let his baby daughter go check for bogies in the dark by herself," Lester declared.

"Jeepers, Lester, I wasn't going to argue. After the events of a couple weeks ago, I think the buddy system is a perfectly good idea when investigating things that go bump in the night," I replied.

A few weeks ago I, along with my twins, Arista and Ian, Lester Duke, our elderly neighbor and my brother, Jacob, were all involved up to our eyeballs in a series of unsettling events. Events that left Lester and Jake with broken arms, several of us with concussions and involved the kidnapping and subsequent return of my twins.

After his release from the hospital, Lester moved in with us temporarily, rather than going to a rehab facility, which he flatly refused to do. The doctor wouldn't release a seventy-something year old with a broken arm and a head injury to go home alone. Before moving home to Blossom Bluff, Missouri to watch over my mom, who has Alzheimer's, and the family farm, I worked as a rehabilitation counselor in Kansas City, Missouri, so we convinced the doctor that staying with my family on the Stonehorse Ranch would be better than a rehab center.

The kids and I have enjoyed having Lester, his tiny dog, Violet, and his elderly Belgium horse, Jackson, stay with us. I, for one, was going to be sad when they returned home, although "home" was the neighboring farm and no more than a half mile away.

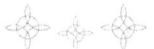

We distracted the small, loud dogs, Sophia and Violet, with some bone-like treats and confined them to the laundry room. Lester and I bundled up in our jackets and grabbed a couple flashlights. Out we went into the dark December chill. We shown our lights around the area nearest the house and car parking area and didn't see anything. Then, as if she were standing next to me whispering in my ear, I heard, *"Fen, you can learn more in the dark and quiet night than you think."* It was my great-grandmother's voice in my head.

"Lester, let's turn the lights off for a moment and listen."

"Okay," Lester flicked off his light.

The sky was glorious with stars and the air so crisp and fresh it tickled my nose. We listened in the dark, which wasn't all that dark since the moon was full, and she was spectacular.

Then I heard it. I began trying to figure out where

JEN KENNING

the tiny sound was coming from.

"Do you hear that, Fen?" Lester asked in a whisper.

"Yes, I do."

"What is it? My old ears aren't as trusty as they used to be," Lester said.

I began walking toward the sound. "I believe it's a kitten, possibly more than one," I said over my shoulder. Lester followed me.

We walked about 75 feet toward the end of the driveway. The tiny sound grew louder as we got closer. There was a second parking area off to the right where we park the old farm truck and the horse trailer. The noise emanated from this region of the property. I tripped on a rock in the graveled driveway and got a rock in my slipper. "Ouch, dammit," I exclaimed. I balanced on one foot and reached for the other to dump out the offending pebble. *Wish I'd had the sense to pull on my boots.*

"You okay?" Lester asked.

He reached for my elbow to steady me. Oh yeah, I'm fine. Just a rock." I looked at Lester's feet, adorned in more suitable Twisted X slip-on style shoes. "Are those comfortable?" I asked motioning to his feet.

"Yep. Easy to get on in a hurry too," he said.

The incessant mewling stopped when I stumbled and talked. We listened, lights off.

"Mew, mew mew!" came from the area underneath the horse trailer. "Mew," from somewhere else.

"Oh dear, there is more than one," I whispered.

"They sound little, too cold for them to be out by themselves," Lester said. "Do you think your barn cat had kittens?"

"Nope, we spay and neuter all cats and dogs we have

living here," I replied.

I clicked my flashlight back on and pointed the beam at the horse trailer. There was a light-colored flash of movement. We picked our way in that direction as quietly as the rocky ground would allow. Tiny eyes reflected in the flashlight beam from the wheel of the trailer tire.

I handed my flashlight to Lester and knelt down to get a better look. A very small white and yellow kitten looked fiercely back at me and hissed. I reached for the kitty. It swiped at my hand with tiny claws. Undeterred, I captured the skin on the back of its neck like a mother cat would. It went mostly limp but continued to hiss and sputter. I stood up and held the little beast up to get a better look. "My, you are a puffed up little ruffian, so very fierce," I whispered to the kitty in what I hoped was a soothing voice.

"What's wrong with its face?" Lester asked, peering over my shoulder.

The kitten's face was a mess. Blood caked around its chin and cheek and the fur was missing in these areas. "It is hurt. We need to get it inside," I said.

As we turned to walk back to the house the kitty struggled and there was a chorus of mewing from further up the driveway.

"This rescue mission isn't complete." I turned toward the noise.

"Sounds like," Lester agreed.

We trudged further up the graveled driveway to the road. We followed the mewing to two more kittens of the same size. Both had abrasions, and neither were all that happy to be picked up. The first kitten had remained anxious but no longer struggled in my hands once its litter mates joined him.

Lester and I stood quietly on the edge of the road, listening for more tiny, furry refugees.

"Do you think there are more?" he asked.

"Jeepers, I hope not. Poor little critters."

After several moments of hearing nothing, we began the trek back to the house. My hands were full of wiggling kittens. Lester held both flashlights and lit the path for us. He opened the door, and we entered the brightly lit kitchen. The dogs were scratching and whining on the other side of the laundry room door. The kittens wiggled harder, and the first one began to hiss again.

Lester and I looked at each other. "Well, this is gonna be fun." I rolled my eyes. He laughed.

I handed the kittens to Lester.

He wasn't all that thrilled about it but took them anyway.

"I'm going to get a basket to corral them in temporarily, be right back." I took off down the hall to my room.

I surveyed my closet. *That will never hold them,* I thought, eyeing the wicker basket and opting for the tall plastic hamper instead. I dumped the contents out on the floor and headed back to the kitchen.

Lester was sitting on the floor, trying to contain the kittens to his lap.

"Fen, they are a mess. All scuffed up, and I think this one has a broken leg." He pointed to the little black one.

Even as he said it, the tiny black kitten hobbled a few steps away from Lester's lap, and the yellow and white one hissed.

"Oh dear, they are a mess!"

During my time as a rehabilitation therapist, I had been required to take several courses in first aid. That was all for humans, but some of the basics transfer to all species. Growing up on a farm had taught me a lot about what to do with injured, sick animals. Sadly, it also taught me that sometimes there wasn't anything you could reasonably do. That was not the case this night.

I gently picked up the black kitten and looked it over. The right front leg was limp from the middle of the leg down and even gentle palpitation of the limb caused the kitten to yowl in pain.

"Okay bitsy, I'm sorry. We *will* get you fixed up." I told it as I set it back down gently. I went to the bathroom and dug through the cabinet for some supplies. I returned to Lester and the kittens with gauze, medical tape, cotton balls and saline solution. Lester watched me.

"Are you going to try to set that tiny leg?" he asked.

"I don't know about setting it. I foresee a trip to the vet for that. I'm going to try to stabilize it enough so that it doesn't get worse. I need a splint."

"Toothpick?" Lester asked.

"Too small. Ahad!" I said as I opened the kitchen drawer that held random objects. We all have one (or more) of those drawers. I grabbed a package of chopsticks. The kind you pick up at Asian restaurants and few people ever use. I opened the package and grabbed the sturdy kitchen shears. I snipped the chopstick into several pieces about an inch long.

I settled myself on the floor next to Lester. "Will you hold the kitty as still as possible for me?"

"I'll do my best. What about these other two?" he asked.

The yellow and white one hissed and skittered away. It went under the built-in desk, above which were several shelves where the cookbooks lived. The third kitten was light grey and was the most content of the three. It sat on Lester's leg and peered around. It had a bare spot on the top of its head. It had bled but was scabbed over. Everything considered, it appeared to be in the best shape.

"That one looks content for now." I pointed at the grey one. "Little Hissy Britches over there will have to wait." I gestured towards the yellow and white one, who watched us with suspicion from under the desk.

Lester held the black kitten as I wrapped the leg with gauze. A couple wraps around and then added the chopstick splints, I wrapped those up. "I don't want the sticks to catch the fur or rub on the skin," I explained.

After taping the gauze in place, I turned my attention to the rest of the kitten. Otherwise, it appeared unscathed. I moistened a cotton ball with saline and wiped its face and ears.

Lester set the kitten down on the floor and it looked at the contraption taped to its leg. It took a tentative step, tried to shake the splint off and stopped. It flopped down on its side with the appendage sticking straight out. Pitiful.

We looked the grey one over and the scab on the top of its head was all we could find. The fur around the wound looked weird. It was uneven, and upon closer inspection looked scorched. I brought the kitten close to my face and took a whiff. There was a burnt hair smell faintly coming from the kitten's wound. An image of a cigar being pressed into the tiny furry skull entered my mind. *Goddess, no!*

"Someone burned this baby!" I said.

Lester's eyes took on a hard glint. "Are you sure?"

"As sure as I can be. The fur smells burnt, and look at the shape of the wound," I said, holding the kitty up to Lester so he could get a closer look. "It looks to be the size and shape of a cigar. Too large to be a cigarette," I concluded.

I purposefully left out the part about the vision. Lester knew the members of my family tended to have some psychic abilities.

I was sure he, at least, suspected my great granny, granny, and Auntie Lou were witches of some kind. Last month when I found him unconscious and bleeding in his barn after a brutal attack, I had used the healing chant passed down to me from these strong women. That, combined with mundane, but uber important first aide likely saved Lester's life.

Lester looked closely at the wound on the furry little head. "Yes, I hate to say it, but that is exactly what it looks like. What kind of a nasty *#@! does that to any creature? I'd like to give that guy a taste of his own medicine."

I cleaned around the wound with saline, then applied a bit of triple antibiotic ointment from the tube I had stuck in my robe pocket as an afterthought. I checked the grey kitten over once more and couldn't discover whether it was a boy or girl. I gave it a snuggle under my chin. "Don't worry little one, no one will ever treat you that way ever again." I promised, and I knew it was true. The grey kitten purred for the first time since it had arrived in my world. I wondered where its mother could be and sent up a silent prayer she was safe from whomever treated her kittens so abusively.

I got up off the floor. I held the grey kitten to my chest. Lester got up grumbling about gravity and old knees.

"I hope we can work on the next one standing up, or at least at the table. I don't think I've got another trip up and down off the floor in me tonight. Getting old stinks." Lester groaned.

"Yeah, but it's better than the alternative," I said with a wink.

"Right you are, lady," he said.

There was a cozy throw draped over the chair by the desk. I grabbed it and nestled it in the bottom of the laundry hamper. I scooped the black kitten up from where it still lay on the floor and placed them both gently inside the hamper. Neither one complained.

"That is an awfully nice blanket to put in a basket of stray kittens. Aren't you worried they'll pee on it?" Lester asked.

"It'll wash. Besides, it is temporary. There are towels and blankets that we keep solely for use with animals, but they are all in the laundry room in a tote, and I am not ready to deal with the dogs yet."

I looked over at the area under the kitchen desk, and the yellow and white kitten appeared to have dozed off. Sitting in the shape of a loaf of bread, with all four feet tucked in under the body, the kitten looked very calm. I got back on the floor and approached the desk quietly on my hands and knees. When I reached under the desk to retrieve the kitten, its eyes popped open. Kitty was instantly on its feet and all puffed up, tail erect, mouth open in a fierce hiss. It would have been more impressive if it had any teeth in its tiny maw. It would have been funny if the cause wasn't sheer terror from how it and its siblings had been treated.

"I know, honey, you've had a hell of a time. Shush, poor baby. You're gonna be okay, and you are safe now." I snatched the little rascal up and brought it against my chest. It hissed and struggled. The wee beastie may have lacked teeth, but there was nothing wrong with its claws. Pinpricks of blood popped out on my hand where the little waif dug in.

I grabbed a kitchen towel off the oven door and wrapped it hastily around the kitten. "Enough of that now, I am *trying* to help you. You have every right to be scared, but there's no need for me to get scarred up," I said. I handed the burrito-shaped kitten bundle to Lester and washed my hands. "I think it's time for some coffee. This one is going to take some time to win over. Would you like to hold the cat or make the coffee?" I asked. Lester handed the packaged kitten back to me.

"I will make the coffee."

The clock on the oven display read 5:53 a.m. I sat at the kitchen island and held the kitty in my lap. Lester and I sipped coffee. He leaned on the other side of the counter. "What do you 'spose happened to these wee cats that they would end up all alone in the driveway in the middle of the night all banged up?"

"I think someone nasty tossed them out of a moving vehicle. Check out the scrapes on this one's little face and chin." I pointed at the marks. "It looks like road rash to me." I stroked the kitten's forehead gently, hoping to further calm it down. An old Braucherei/PowWow chant my Auntie Lou had taught me popped into my head.

My great-grandmother and grandmother were witches, both were known to practice PowWow. The *witch gene,* as my father used to call it, skipped my mother for reasons I never understood. Powwow is an old Pennsylvania Dutch term for a practitioner of Folk Magick. Today the term "Braucherie" is used instead. This was our family tradition, and my Auntie Lou taught me the methods when I was little.

The chant I was thinking of was originally meant to protect one from aggressive, possibly rabid, dogs. Like most chants or spells it can be modified to suit the circumstances. Although Lester had been our neighbor since well before I was born and surely knew my grandmother was a locally renowned *wisewoman,* I was not sure about openly chanting over this kitten in front of him. *Silent it is.*

"Lester, are you ready to help me clean this wee beastie up?"

Lester drank the last of his coffee and put his cup in the sink. "Sure Fen, no time like the present."

I handed the kitty off to Lester and grabbed a warm, moist washcloth. Lester held the towel-wrapped kitty on the counter as I began to wash the abrasions on its face as well as the gash on his little chin. Silently, I repeated:

> *Kitten, hold thy nose to the ground*
> *Goddess hath made thee*
> *And me a friend.*
> *As I Will So Mote it Be*
> *(Modified from Hexcraft by Silver Raven Wolf)*

Kitty squeaked once while I cleaned the gash but was otherwise still. Lester, to his credit, spoke in a soft voice to the kitten. He told it what a brave kitten it was and that we were trying to help it.

I put some antibiotic ointment on the cuts. "Okay, all done. You can put him in the hamper with the others. Thank you for staying up and helping me get them situated."

Lester placed the kitten in the hamper with the other two. "They fell asleep, I suppose they are hungry though. What you got to feed something that small? They can't even be weaned yet."

"That's the next hurdle. Straight cow's milk isn't good for them. I will pick up some kitten food later in town, but for now a bit of watered-down canned cat food with some plain yogurt mixed in will have to do."

I drank the rest of my coffee, which had gotten cold. I selected a can of Isabella's food from under the counter. Chicken pate would likely be the most digestible choice, so I chose it and got to mixing breakfast for three weary, beat-up kittens.

CHAPTER 2

My 15-year-old twins, Ian and Arista, emerged from their rooms in a rush at 6:45a.m. Their normal morning greetings of "Hey Mom, Morning Mom, what's for breakfast?" were abbreviated when they stopped short upon seeing the kittens.

The kittens had finished their food moments before and were fumbling around next to their dish. The yellow and white one, who I had begun to think of as Elliot, stood over the black kitten and puffed up, hissing at the kids. *The protector.*

"Whoa! Kittens!" Ian exclaimed.

"Aww, they're adorable, where'd they come from?" Arista reached for "Elliot," and got a scratch on the finger. "Oh my, you're a feisty one."

I placed a hastily assembled breakfast of egg sandwiches and milk on the kitchen island and related the story of how the kittens came to be in our kitchen, their injuries, and the care I, with Lester's help, had provided.

By the time I was done with the story, it was time

for Ian to head out to the end of the driveway to catch the school bus. He bade me and Lester g'bye and told Arista he'd see her later at school. It was Thursday, the day Arista was scheduled to spend the morning volunteering at the nursing home.

I picked up the breakfast dishes. "I'll drop y'all off at the nursing home and go do the grocery shopping and errands."

While Arista did her volunteer work, Lester would visit with his wife, Mary. She had been in the nursing home for a little over a year after a stroke left her with mobility issues. Lester went up to visit her every day until a few weeks ago when he was attacked at his home. Lester's arm was in a cast, and coupled with the fact his truck was a manual transmission which had prevented him from keeping the daily schedule, he still managed to visit four to five days a week.

"Okay Mom, I'll get my stuff ready to go." Arista headed down the hallway.

"Are you going to take the kittens to the vet or shelter or something?" Lester asked, as he finished his last bite of toast and put his plate in the sink.

"I'll call the veterinarian's office and see when we can get in. The kittens have been through so much already, I can't stand the thought of them going to the shelter. Besides the nearest no-kill shelter is sixty-five miles away. They can stay here for now. How much trouble can they be?"

My phone rang, it was Ian. I answered it. "Hey, honey, are you okay? Did you forget something?"

"I'm all good, Mom, but when the bus drove on up the road about a mile, I saw a tabby cat and a kitten on the side of the road. They had been hit and didn't make it. I thought you would want to know since maybe they were related to those three y'all found. I gotta go, see you later." Ian clicked off the call.

I poured myself a cup of coffee in a travel mug and related what Ian told me to Lester.

"It looks more and more like someone tossed them out of a moving car," Lester said. "Such a shame that people are cruel to little animals."

Violet came into the kitchen and stood on her hind legs. She pawed at Lester and so he picked her up. She wore her doggy sweater. Arista must have put in on her in preparation to leave. Lester took Violet to visit Mary in the home. Well-behaved dogs were always welcome there.

The drive to the nursing home and subsequent grocery shopping were uneventful. I called the vet and was told they could see the kittens at 11 a.m. so I hustled home to drop off the groceries and pick up the kittens. When I got to the house, Yvonne, a long-time friend of my mother's, arrived to pick up Mom and take her to the Senior Center. This had become an almost daily event.

My mom suffered from Alzheimer's, as well as the after effects of a traumatic brain injury, and could no longer live on her own. This was the reason the kids and I moved back to our family farm in the little community of Blossom Bluff, Missouri.

Fortunately, Mom still had her mobility and needed very little help to dress and with her hygiene activities. We didn't dare let her cook. Mom almost started a fire when she forgot about a frying pan full of bacon. Thus, the reason for me to leave Kansas City and my job there as a Rehabilitation Counselor in the rear-view mirror. I had no regrets, and if the kids missed city life, they hid it well.

"Good morning, Yvonne, Mom, I see you're heading out. Is it a Senior Center Day or do you have something else planned?" I grabbed as many bags of groceries as possible to carry in the house. I really hate to make more than one trip if I can avoid it.

"Hi, Fen."

Yvonne opened the car door for my mom.

"Good morning, honey. Yes, we are going to the Senior Center. We have to help with the float," Mom said cheerfully.

I looked at Yvonne to gauge the accuracy of my mother's statement. You never knew for sure with Alzheimer's patients. "Float?"

"Yep, that's right! Instead of the usual activities, everyone is going to be painting the float for the Christmas Parade. Everyone is in a rush to get it finished since the parade is the day after tomorrow. It should be good fun," Yvonne said.

She and Mom smiled in a way that made me wonder if they were up to something. They left in Yvonne's car.

After I put the groceries away and opened the laundry room door, I expected to find the kittens tucked up in the hamper asleep. Nope.

"Oh my stars! What have you been doing? How did you get out?" I asked the room at large, which was a disaster. The kittens scattered when I opened the door, except for the one with the broken leg, who hobbled as fast as possible back to the laundry hamper, now on its side.

They had managed to tip it over as well as the trash can. Our muck boots, once neatly lined up on the drying mat were now knocked over. There was a tiny yellow and white kitten butt sticking out of one of Ian's boots.

"I can see you, you little hellion." The grey kitten was attacking and scattering a lump of dryer lint on the floor, presumably out of the trash they knocked over.

He/she (they were too small to tell yet) was completely undeterred by my scolding. I checked the time, 9:25 a.m. Sophia, my small fuzzy dog of indeterminate parentage, poked her head into the room, saw the mess and looked up at me as if to say, "It wasn't me this time."

"Come on, Sophie, you go outside for a bit." I closed the door to the laundry room. I let her out and refilled my travel mug with coffee. It was time to gather the kittens into a pet taxi for the trip to the vet's office. I went into the laundry room and shut the door behind me. It wouldn't do for a kitten to escape into the main part of the house.

I tucked the grey and black kittens into the crate without difficulty. It took 20 minutes to get the yellow and white one, who I now thought of as Houdini instead of Elliot. I extricated it from behind the dryer, where he sat and hissed at me. "I'm quite sure it was you who caused this ruckus." *Houdini the Hellion. Has a ring to it.* Once I was able to retrieve the kitten, I held him close to my chest and he/she began to purr. *Little turd.*

I pulled into the parking lot at the Blossom Bluff

Animal Hospital with moments to spare. The kittens had meowed loudly the entire way. It made the ten-mile jaunt seem like fifty. I sat in the waiting room with the cage of kittens at my feet. The receptionist said the doctor was running a bit behind. A tiny yellow and white paw popped through the bars of the pet taxi and snagged my pant leg. The kitten let out a terse sounding yowl. The gentleman across the room, waiting with a bull mastiff looked up from his phone and frowned. The mastiff grinned as a string of drool slid down from his chin and plopped onto the floor. The guy rolled his eyes, pulled a small towel out of his pocket and wiped the dog's chin and the floor.

I dislodged the tiny claws from my denim cuff and whispered, "Shush now, you're okay."

"Mew!"

A flurry of activity erupted from the right side of the office. A woman came out with a small, white, perfectly groomed dog. The woman was about 5'4" and wore a dark blue skirt with a blue and white striped jacket. Her blue pumps looked expensive. I had never seen her before. A guy was standing in the doorway the woman had exited. The woman said something about when should she bring the dog back. The guy, who I noticed was wearing a dark green lab coat, spoke.

"Miss Vanderkamp, your dog is perfectly healthy, bring her back in a year for her annual check-up. Just keep up with her flea, tick, and heartworm meds."

"But Doctor, what if she throws up again?" the woman said, leaning in toward the doctor.

"If that happens, call the office, the receptionist will get you an appointment."

The guy stepped back and shut the door. The woman

tossed her head and turned. Our eyes met, and for a moment, I had the strangest feeling that I would be seeing more of her.

"That is a cute dog, what kind is it?" I asked with a smile.

"It's a Bichon Frise, her name is Imelda." She tossed her head again.

The dog stretched its leash to get closer to the kittens' crate. She sniffed the crate, and I held my hand down so she could sniff the back of it.

"Hi, Melly, what a good girl you are!"

"Her name is IMELDA, not Melly," the woman said, as if the last word tasted particularly bad. She pulled on the leash and headed for the main door of the clinic.

I briefly considered hollering, "Bye, Melly," just to be contrary since the woman was kind of obnoxious, but the receptionist called my name.

"Right this way, Ms. Stern. Doctor Spencer will be right with you," the receptionist said.

I picked up the cat carrier and headed for the door leading to the exam rooms located in the rear of the building. "Dr. Spencer? Where is Dr. Johnson? He has been our family vet for years."

"Dr. Johnson is in South America doing some missionary work, he'll be back in about eight weeks. I'm sorry you didn't know. Dr. Spencer is filling in and doing a good job. Do you want to reschedule so you can see Dr. Johnson?"

The receptionist, whose name tag read, Julie, asked as she opened the door for me. "No, that's okay, these little ones shouldn't wait that long. Thank you for getting us in today to see the doctor." I walked through the doorway and Julie showed me to an exam room. She closed the door of the room with the assurance that the doc would be in momentarily.

The kittens and I waited about ten minutes before the exam room door opened again. We were all fidgety. I had to pee, and I suspected they were hungry or bored or both, *same as kids.*

The guy in the dark green lab coat came in. He had a stethoscope slung around his neck and a slightly flustered air about him. I noticed that his left hand was sporting a bandage on the area where the thumb meets the wrist. I didn't recall seeing it earlier when he ushered the woman in the fancy suit out. I noticed he was tall, a bit over six feet. The lab coat didn't hide the abundance of muscles that made his t-shirt stretch.

CHAPTER 3

"Hello, I'm Doctor Spencer. Julie tells me you have some kittens needing attention. I hope you brought their mother, too."

"Hi, Dr. Spencer, I am Fen Stern. I don't have the mother. I found these kittens last night."

"Well, let's see what we have here." He reached for the cat carrier with his left hand and winced.

"What happened there?" I pointed to the bandaged hand as I picked up the carrier and set it up on the large, stainless steel examination table. "Did that mastiff I saw in the waiting room tag you?"

"Nope, that is Otis and he's a good boy. I really shouldn't say, but it was the tiny white dog that got me. It's not too bad, though it is the reason you had to wait for me. I took a few minutes to clean the wound and wrap it up."

"Perfectly understandable." I reached inside the carrier and grasped the grey kitten. Of course, the moment the door was open, Houdini, the Hellion, scooted out and took off. The kitten didn't understand the table was about three feet off the ground, or that it is nearly impossible to stop quickly on stainless steel. The kitten slid right off the end of the table and would have hit the floor if Dr. Spencer hadn't been quick enough to catch him.

"Hi there, little guy." Dr. Spencer held his captive up for a better look. "You are going to be a handful, aren't ya? What happened to his face?"

"I'm not sure but have a theory that its road rash." I gave doc the cliff notes version of finding the kittens and included Ian's discovery of the two cats in the road within a mile of our home. "I can only figure that someone tossed them out of their car."

Dr. Spencer listened to the story as he looked over Houdini and placed him on the floor. He held out both hands for the grey kitten I held. When he saw the round wound on top of its head, his jaw clenched.

"This one has been burned?"

"That's what I thought, too. I hate that they were dumped, but sadly even that might be better than wherever they were before. I dearly hope whoever treated them this way gets their just desserts." I didn't bother to hide the anger that I felt towards the anonymous abuser.

Doctor Spencer nodded. "Yeah, no kidding." He recleaned the wound and put a different type of salve on it. "The triple antibiotic you used is fine in a pinch, but this is a silver alginate compound, and it will speed healing. I will send this tube home with you." He gently placed the grey kitten on the floor with its sibling. They scurried around playing kitten games. Doc took a small fuzzy ball out of his lab coat pocket and tossed it down between the kittens.

Aww, that is sweet he carries cat toys around in his pocket. Dr. Johnson never did that. I shook off the thought and reached into the cat carrier and brought out the black kitty with the broken leg. Once placed on the cold table, the kitten mewed and tried to hobble back towards me but couldn't get any traction with the splinted leg.

The doctor gaped at the kitten, the leg and looked at me. "Who wrapped the leg up?"

"I did," I replied unable to meet the doctor's eyes. I felt self-conscious and hoped watching the kittens at my feet was a sufficient cover.

He began his examination of the kitten and explained that he would need to unwrap the leg to assess the injury and may want to get an Xray.

Dr. Spencer touched my arm lightly. "Hey, you did good stabilizing it. Are those chopsticks?"

I looked up and smiled. "Yep" *That was articulate Fen, geez.*

"Very clever. I'll be right back, I'm going to grab an Xray of the leg so we know what we are dealing with for sure." Doc started to open the door to leave but changed his mind when Houdini aimed his body at the crack. "Oh no you don't, I knew you were trouble."

He picked up the wayward yellow and white kitten and handed it to me with a grin. I hugged the kitten to my chest as doc left the room. *"Trouble" maybe that is your name.*

"Mrow!" He shook his tiny head and grabbed my thumb with claws extended.

"Dang it, cat, stop that." *Evidently it doesn't like that name. Oh well, something else will come to mind.*

I picked up the grey kitten and placed them both back into the carrier with their ball so we wouldn't have any escapes when doc returned. I ventured into the hallway and found the receptionist.

She was on the phone. "Yes, sir, we can get you in as an emergency, come on in.

"Did you say someone beat your dog?

"That's awful, you should file a police report.

"The cops will do more than you think, animal abuse is a crime."

I planned to ask her to let doc know I stepped out to use the lady's room and the kittens were contained, but the part of the conversation I could hear caught my attention. I hovered near the desk until the receptionist's call was concluded.

Doc wasn't back from Xraying the black kitten yet when I returned to the exam room. I let the grey kitten and "Elliot Houdini Trouble," out of the crate and sat down on the floor to play with them. Doc returned with the black kitten. He had already re-wrapped the broken leg. I stood up and dusted off my jeans. The clinic was clean, but there is always the ubiquitous animal hair and dust. "What's the scoop on his little leg, Doc?"

Doc handed me the kitten and put the Xray up on the back-lit holder on the wall. He pointed at a tiny white line in the middle of the leg. "It's a clean break, not displaced, and I wrapped it up the same way you had it. Kittens are resilient and this one will heal fast. We want to keep it wrapped and stable for ten days."

We talked a bit about nutrition requirements for the

kitties. Doc estimated their age at five weeks, and his best guess on the gender of each one. He carried the pet taxi, escorted me back to the waiting room then handed the taxi to me.

"It was nice meeting you, Mrs. Stern, I will see you in three weeks for a follow up appointment. In the meantime just call as needed."

"Thank you, Doctor Spencer,"

I noticed the time, realized I was late and hurried to my truck, a four door King Cab, four-wheel drive Dodge. It was a lot of truck for running simple errands. Right after the kids and I moved down from Kansas City, the motor went out in my Toyota Camry. It was older, and since I wouldn't be commuting every day any longer, I chose to sell it for parts and had not replaced it yet. The big Dodge truck belonged to my daddy and it reminded me of him every time I drove it. When Mom and Dad had the wreck that killed him and left Mom with a Traumatic Brain Injury, they were in their Dodge Caravan, it was a total loss.

As I was pulled out of the vet's office parking lot, a little blue car came screeching into the parking lot. *They're comin' in hot. Wonder if that is the guy from the phone call. Somebody beat his dog, what is wrong with people.*

The vet appointment took a bit longer than anticipated, and I was late to pick up Arista and Lester from the nursing home. Arista had to be back at school and in her first class at 12:45. They were waiting outside when I pulled in and stopped in front of the building. Lester climbed in the front seat and Arista clambered into the rear seat beside the cat carrier. She began playing with the kittens through the cage bars. I told them all about the kittens' doctor visit on the short drive to the high school. We pulled into the parking lot at 12:43 and Arista jumped out and took off. She grumbled something about the new Superintendent being really picky.

I was famished, but Lester had eaten lunch with his wife, Mary, at the nursing home. I opted for a quick stop at the sub shop. A six-inch club on wheat would tide me over until supper.

It was 1:35 p.m. by the time we arrived back at our family home. The house was not the original house on the property. Daddy built it about 12 years ago. I remember asking him why he was building such a large house since all of us kids would move out soon. He told me, "Might need the room someday. Your Auntie Lou isn't the only one that gets "feelings."

We were barely inside, and Lester asked, "You want some coffee? Feels like this day is longer than the rest."

"That's because we were on kitten search and rescue duty at four o'clock this morning. Yes please, I want some coffee." I put the pet taxi on the floor and let Sophia and Violet, who danced the, oh we're glad to see you but we have to pee, let us out dance, around my feet.

I got the kittens food and water and turned them loose in the laundry room, then took a seat at the kitchen island. It didn't take long to wolf down the sub sandwich and the coffee that followed was a relaxing break from the day's events.

Lester took his coffee and headed out to the machine

shop to tinker with the antique tractor. He and Ian were rehabilitating it, and they planned to drive it in the Blossom Bluff Christmas Parade, which was scheduled for the day after tomorrow.

My phone roared like a tiger, alerting a text message.

"Hey, wanna ride tomorrow?" It was from my friend Jana.

"Sure, when? Where?"

"Dusty Ole Knob at 10 a.m.?"

"K, see u there."

The rest of the day passed rapidly into evening. The kids arrived home from school, followed by Mom. Yvonne agreed to stay for supper. We all sat down to beef stew and biscuits.

I had to convince Arista to leave the kittens in the laundry room overnight. She lobbied to have them sleep in her room, but I won because I'm the mom.

"Arista, we need to make sure they are accustomed to using their litter box before we make their world any larger. Besides they are much too small to be running loose in the house."

"Fine. I just feel bad because they are all alone and someone was mean to them." She huffed as she held the little grey furball and tickled his tummy.

The yellow and white one began to climb my leg as if I were a tree.

A cat growled and hissed, an icy wind blew and an engine roared. A thud, a cry, the coppery smell of blood. It was dark.

I awoke frantic. I wondered where my kids were.

Did I smell blood? No that was a dream. I want to check anyway. I crawled out of bed and donned my robe and slippers. It was five a.m. I peeked into both my twins' rooms, both were present and sleeping peacefully. I peeked in on Mom, too. She was muttering in her sleep.

"Big truck, bad man, Gibbs will get you, bad man. Poor kitty," followed by a snore.

I stifled a laugh, Mom's preoccupation with her NCIS hero, Leroy Jethro Gibbs was adorable. *We both dreamed about cats. I guess our respective minds were working out our angst about our newest houseguests.*

I considered the time and sighed. I was up for the day and put on a pot of coffee. After popping a made-ahead breakfast casserole in the oven, I set the timer and headed for a long hot shower.

When I returned to the kitchen an hour later, fully dressed for the day in Levis and layered shirts, Arista sat on the floor in the kitchen playing with the kittens as Lester drank coffee.

"Good morning. Wow Arista, you are up early!"

"Quality kitten time. The oven timer went off and the food looked done, so I took it out. Hope that was right." Arista tossed the fuzzy ball across the floor and the kittens took out after it.

"Perfect, thank you."

Ian arrived in the kitchen, hair still wet from his shower, and tossed his backpack on the floor near the door. "G' morning y'all, oh is that Swiss Eggs?" he asked. He snatched a plate off the counter and filled it with the egg casserole. The yellow and white kitten ran up his leg in a flash and tried to stick his nose in Ian's plate. "No ya don't, little buddy. Geez you climb like a monkey, a ravenous monkey." He handed the kitten off to his sister.

Arista secured the kittens in the laundry room and fixed herself a plate of breakfast. "Mom, do you remember today I'm staying after school to try out for the new softball team? Zoey's mom said she would bring me home, that's still okay, right?"

"Yes, I remember talking about it. Softball in December, though?" I mixed up food for the kittens.

"Since it is a new program for our school, try outs are earlier and the girls that make the team will have a different PE class for conditioning starting in January. I hope I make the team, Zoey and Brandy too. I know Brandy will, she is really good. She played at her old school in Springfield." Arista rinsed her plate and stuck it in the dishwasher.

The kids left for school. I headed to the barn to get my mule ready for the trail ride

I looked forward to a day on the trails. November had been unseasonably snowy, but December was mild and dry so far. Missouri weather is odd that way.

BB, which is short for Blondie Boy (Arista named him when she was five years old) is a palomino gaited mule. He is the smartest equine I've ever encountered. It wouldn't be a stretch to say he helped save our lives last month when the kids and I were held prisoner.

He snorted softly when I entered the barn and readily accepted the apple-flavored cookie from my hand. I fixed him half his breakfast ration and brushed him down. Once he finished with his food and was saddled, we commenced to the horse trailer. I'd hooked it up last night so it would be ready to go. Dusty Ole Knob, where I was to meet my friend was about twenty miles away, so we needed to get moving.

My friend, Jana Smith, is kind, funny and fiercely protective of our community. You see, she is also a deputy sheriff.

We knew each other from school, but she was a couple grades behind me, so we didn't hang out together back then. The events of last month threw us together and she began to date my younger brother Jacob.

Jana was parked at the trail head when I arrived. She had her horse ready to go. I hopped out of my truck. "Hey, Jana, sorry if I'm late." I opened my trailer and BB walked out like he owned the place.

"Good morning! You're right on time. I got here early so I could let Chester settle down." She patted her horse, a chestnut-colored gelding. We called him "Chester the Jester" because he could be a bit goofy at times.

"I'm glad we made time to do this today, couldn't ask for better weather!" I climbed on BB.

"I agree one hundred percent," Jana said.

We rode up the winding trail. We chatted about everything and nothing. Sometimes we rode in companionable silence as we listened to the sounds nature offered. The air was crisp and fresh, the temperature warmed up nicely as the sun shone brightly through the naked trees. After about an hour it warmed up to about 60 degrees. I peeled off my jacket and tied it around my waist.

"When we get to the top, do you wanna stop and have a snack? I brought a thermos of coffee and some pastries from Cones and Scones," Jana said.

"You're awesome! Heck, yeah, I'm always up for coffee and sweets."

The trail up to Dusty Ole Knob took about two hours. It's not that the knob is so high, the trail winds and meanders along. It is part of the Ozark Mountains, which are not tall, compared to the likes of the Rockies or the Appalachian Mountains, but they are still rugged and littered with rocks. A winding trail is safer than one that goes straight up or straight down. The top of this knob is flat and mostly bare. I always thought it looked like Mother Nature had whacked the top of it off, kind of like you might level a cup of sugar.

Once we reached the top of the knob, we dismounted. Jana tied Chester to a log. I never bother to tie BB up. If he really wanted to go somewhere, no tie would stop him, and I knew he wouldn't leave me without a good reason. It felt good to stretch my legs and Jana said as much.

We sat on a log, with our coffee in hand and an open box of pastries between us.

"BOOM!"

CHAPTER 4

We both jumped, Chester lost his mind and pulled back on his tie. He shrieked. Even BB startled. My coffee went flying and Jana, who had just taken a drink, spewed coffee down her brown Carhart vest. She ran to calm Chester down before he broke free, and I put my hands on BB's neck.

"What the heck was that?" I asked.

"Sounded like an explosion." She stroked her horse to soothe him.

"Where? The way sound carries and bounces off the hills it could be miles away." I peered around.

"Look there." She pointed to a plume of black smoke some distance away and a few hills over. "What is over that way?"

It took me a moment to get my bearings, and I dug in my saddlebag for my map. Technology made paper maps all but obsolete in cities but out here, where cell signals are spotty at best, it was hard to beat a trusty map. The caveat is that you have to figure out where North is.

I sighed and pointed at the map. "We are here. I can't figure out what direction that is." The sun was directly overhead and no help whatsoever. "The trail was so curvy, and my directions are so confused, I only know how to get back to the trucks."

Jana dug in her bag and came up with a compass and her cell phone. "I need to call this in if I can get a signal." She handed me the compass and began walking slowly around. She held her phone up to try to catch a bar or two.

I studied the map and the compass and decided the smoke was to the east of our location, the trouble was nothing of any consequence was noted on the map. No town, notable buildings or businesses. We were in the boonies after all.

Jana found a slight signal and explained what she knew (not much) to the dispatcher. She peered at the map I'd spread on the log and gave me a quizzical look. I pointed and then held up both hands with a shrug in the classic -darned if I know- gesture.

Jana told the dispatcher it would take us some time to get back down to the trail head, so they better send a patrol out to look around. They settled on a general area and dispatch radioed the volunteer fire department to be on the lookout.

We hurried to pick up our trash and mounted up for the trek back down the mountain. BB took off with a fast walk, smooth as silk. Chester had some trouble keeping up. Ninety minutes later we arrived back at the parking area and wasted no time loading the equine.

Curiosity overwhelmed me, and I decided to follow Jana in the direction of the explosion. We headed east and then turned north. I could see a trail of smoke rise, though it wasn't nearly as thick as it had been.

When we arrived on the scene, two volunteer fireman were there and had extinguished a few small brush fires that had popped up. Deputy Clyde Young, Jana's coworker and one of my least favorite people in the world, was also on scene.

Jana and I walked over to where the guys stood. Deputy Young turned and glared at us as we approached.

"Fenreya Stern, don't you have anything better to do than stick your nose into official police business?"

I put on my most brilliant smile, fake though it was. "Why no, Deputy Young, at the moment I don't have anything better to do. I came along to see if I could be of any help."

Young started to reply.

"No you—" Jana cut him off.

"She's with me ,Clyde, what have you found out?" Jana said.

"Some old RV blew up." He gestured at the smoking pile of what appeared to have once been a motor home. "Probably an old propane tank or something," he said.

"What ignited it?" Jana asked as she looked at Young and the firemen in turn.

The firemen shrugged. Deputy Young hooked his thumbs in his overtaxed belt and said, "Oh prolly just some kids screwing around, smoking dope or something."

"Some kids smoking dope. That's your theory? Have you checked for bodies? Injured persons? Have you called Sheriff Peters or maybe the Fire Chief?" Jana's voice rose and her frustration with the other deputy's obvious ineptitude began to show.

The firemen shifted around, looking uncomfortable and one of them pulled out his phone and dialed. I presumed he might be calling his chief.

Deputy Young's face was getting red. "No I hadn't got around to all that yet. You think you're so smart. Every time we pull up on a scene, we don't have to carry on like it's one of those cop shows on TV."

"Yes, Clyde, we do. It is our job, we are cops and there are procedures. That's why those shows are called procedurals." She dragged the words out with emphasis.

I had to rub my face to hide my amusement.

She continued, "Oh, never mind, I'll call the Sheriff."

I walked back over to the horse trailers, ostensibly to check on the equine, but I wanted to avoid any further interactions with Clyde. Jana came over to me after she got off the phone with Sheriff John Peters.

"Fen, I'm going to be here for an hour or so. I want to make sure the scene is secure and be here when the sheriff gets here. I hope there was no one in that thing when it went up."

"Yeah, no kidding. Would you like me to take Chester home with me so he doesn't have to spend all that time in the trailer? You can swing up later after you are done. Or even tomorrow and pick him up," I said.

"That would be great, thank you. He is still a young horse, and he has had a stressful day." Jana smiled and headed for the rear of her trailer.

Dark set in by the time I arrived home and unloaded

BB and Chester. Ian was already home from school and came out to give me a hand.

"Hey Mom, why is Jana's horse here? Is Jana okay?"

"We are horse sitting until she comes by later to get him. Jana is stuck at a potential crime scene." I dusted off my hands and handed the truck keys to Ian.

The twins were only fifteen years old with learner's permits, but as is the case for most country kids, they had been driving around the farm for a couple years.

"How about you park the trailer for me, and I'll go start some supper?"

"Sure thing, Mom. Crime scene?" Ian took the keys and raised an eyebrow.

"Yeah, it might be nothing, but Jana had to wait for the sheriff to arrive. I'll fill you in later," I replied over my shoulder as I headed for the house.

I popped a large meatloaf and a potato casserole in the oven, both of which I had made ahead of time. I saw no sign of Lester. I figured he was in the machine shed, tinkering, and there was a note from Yvonne. It said she would have Mom home by six p.m.

I plopped down in my favorite chair in the family room and pulled up the Kindle app on my phone. I was to a good part when the kitchen erupted with activity. Yvonne and my mom bustled in, followed by Arista.

"Mom, guess what! I made the team! So did Brandy, and OMG, she is so good. She has her own bat and everything. She hit the ball out twice during tryouts!" Arista said with excited, animated hand waves.

"That's wonderful, honey, congratulations! Wow, she must have quite a swing," I said.

"What about Zoey, did she make the team?"

Ian tried to sound nonchalant, but we all knew he had a crush on Zoey.

"No, bless her heart, she can't hit the broad side of a barn. Don't you dare tell her I said that," Arista answered.

"You kids get your homework and chores done. Supper will be ready in about thirty minutes." I got up from my chair and headed for the kitchen.

We sat down to supper when lights showed through the kitchen window. Jana drove in and stopped her truck. She hopped out. Sophie and Violet greeted her at the kitchen door. Both dogs loved her.

"Hey everyone!" Jana greeted dogs and humans alike.

Through the chorus of "Hey Jana, how's it going and good to see you," I asked Arista to grab another place setting. "Would you like some supper?" I asked.

"Heck yes, your meatloaf is legendary." She grinned as she washed up in the kitchen sink.

The dinner conversation was primarily Yvonne and Mom who told us about the parade float entry the Senior Center sponsored in a partnership with the nursing home.

Arista chimed in with news of the parade entry for the Future Farmers of America, which she belonged to. Ian and Lester, not to be outdone, told us that the antique tractor they had been refurbishing would be ready to go to the parade tomorrow. They also admitted they needed some help with the logistics of getting it to town and back home after the parade. Evidently the idea of that old of a tractor traveling that distance was unrealistic.

"Well gentlemen, that is why we have a trailer. How

about I drop you guys and the tractor off at the beginning of the parade route, then I will park the truck and trailer down at the lower end of the city park?" I began to clear the table.

Ian and Lester shared a smile. "That would be great Fen," Lester said.

"Yeah Mom, awesome, but how will you get back up to the parade start if you park down there? That is a long walk, and it is apt to be crowded." Ian rose to help his sister collect the dirty dishes.

"I plan on riding BB in the parade. Since I now need to pull the flat trailer with the tractor on it, BB can ride in the bed of the truck. He has done it before and doesn't mind it."

Jana shook her head. "Your mule amazes me. I hope someday Chester is chill enough to just load up in the back of a truck and go somewhere without a fuss." She picked up her plate and took it to the kitchen.

I laughed. "BB is a special mule, but I've seen plenty of other mules and horses ride in the back of trucks and even on flat trailers, not that I think it is particularly safe. There should at least be sides on the conveyance."

"Jana, are you riding Chester in the parade tomorrow?" Arista asked.

"No, Chester isn't quite ready for that yet. Besides I volunteered to help with traffic control since the City PD is a bit shorthanded."

Jana said good night to everyone and made to leave. Ian and Lester went out to help her retrieve Chester from our barn and get him loaded, along with his saddle and so forth.

Yvonne reminded us she would return at eight a.m.

to pick Mom up for the parade.

I fed the kittens and sat down on the floor in the laundry room to play with them for a while. *Gosh you guys are cute. I need to figure out a different place to keep you, I hate that you are in here by yourselves.*

They wrestled around and intermittently played with their fuzzy toy until the little black one discovered my toes. Suddenly I was their favorite toy. *Kittens are addictive.* I wiggled my fingers at the grey one, who sat up on its haunches and batted at my hand with tiny paws. The effort put it off balance and it toppled over, only to be pounced on by the yellow and white one. I was still laughing at them when I heard Ian call from the kitchen.

"Hey Mom, Lester and I switched trailers for you already, so we don't have to do it in the morning. I'm going to bed, love you."

Arista poked her head in the laundry room. "Hey Mom, can I please take the kittens to my room? I will keep the door shut. Look, they are using their box really well. It's just they are so little and all alone. Pleeeeaase, Momma."

I looked at my daughter and at the tiny kittens. I caved. "Okay, but any mess they make, or chaos they create will be your responsibility. Don't get attached to them. Just because some scumbag tossed out a Crazy Cat Lady Starter Pack at our house does not mean we are keeping them. We must get them healed up and off to a good start so proper homes can be found." As I made this declaration the wee yellow and white one pounced on my foot and began to climb my leg. *Oh dear.*

My phone roared like a tiger, alerting me to an

incoming text message from my brother Jacob.

"Hey sis, I'm coming in tonight, flight just landed. Don't wait up."

Jacob's younger than me by a couple of years. He's a gifted businessman and a genius with all manner of technology. He has lived in California for several years but has come home to Missouri more often now that he has begun to date Jana. It started last month during the nasty business in the weeks leading up to Thanksgiving. Their getting together was a silver lining in that dark cloud.

"K. Door's unlocked. There is leftover meatloaf in the fridge. Be safe."

"Cool, thanks, sis. G'night."

CHAPTER 5

A cat growled and hissed, an icy wind blew and an engine roared. A thud, a cry, the coppery smell of blood. It was dark. There were angry voices coming from shadowy figures, two maybe three? A flash of pink, the smell of blood.

I awoke with a start. "What the heck?" It was dark in my room, and I felt, rather than saw Sophia wag her tail. Isabella, a cat not to be disturbed by the middle of the night musings of a mere human, did not move. "It was the same dream, almost.

"Crap. I should write it down." Sophie wagged her tail. I checked the time, two a.m. "Nope, not doin' it." I rolled over and went back to sleep. I made a semi-conscious decision to get in touch with my inner cat.

BANG! BANG! BANG! Sounded on my door.

"Mom, wake up, we are going to be late!" Ian shouted.

Blast it all. "What time is it?" I hollered back as my feet hit the floor and I began to scurry around for my robe and slippers.

"It's nine o'clock, are you okay? You never sleep this late!"

I opened the door. "Oh, yeah, I'm fine, a restless night, I guess." I went to the kitchen where Lester placed a steaming cup of coffee with cream in front of me. *Bless him.*

"Sorry, fellas I will kick it into high gear after I get this down." I took a drink of the divine potion, willing it to open my senses and get my brain moving.

Lester chuckled and Ian said, "It's cool, Mom, we have to be lined up at the parade route at 11:30 a.m. We already loaded the tractor. Uncle Jacob helped."

Jacob strode into the kitchen, grinning like a fool. He was on his phone.

"Okay, hon, I'll see you there." He ended his call.

Arista walked into the kitchen, "Ooh, Uncle Jake has a girlfriend."

Ian chimed in with, "Jacob and Jana, sittin' in a tree."

They both made kissing noises. Lester and I snickered at the kids' antics and Jacob's facial expression.

Is my baby brother, hot jock in high school, B.M.O.C. in college, really blushing?

"What? Are you people in kindergarten?" Jacob headed down the hallway in a huff.

I downed my coffee. "I need to hustle. We can leave in twenty minutes. Arista, will you feed the kittens?"

"Already done, Mom," Arista called.

While I got dressed, I remembered BB. *Shoot, I've got to get him ready to go, too, I shouldn't have overslept. Fen you dingbat.*

My phone roared with a text message from my

Auntie Lou, "Everything is in perfect timing, even when it isn't." *Auntie Lou, Queen of the Cryptic Text Messages.*

Fifteen minutes later I rushed outside and found my beloved mule, BB already wearing his saddle and standing patiently in the back of my truck. "You're a good mule BB, we'll leave in a minute." Ten minutes later we piled into my truck. "Where is Jacob?" I asked.

"He already left. He wanted to drive himself so he could meet his honey," Ian said.

"Who tacked up BB and loaded him for me?"

"Jacob and I saddled him. Between us we have two good arms." Lester chuckled and waved his cast. "BB loaded himself. We no more than got the saddle strapped on him when he walked over to the truck. He stood there looking at us until Jacob dropped the tailgate. BB hopped in and has been standing there ever since. That mule blows my mind." Lester concluded, shaking his head.

"Thank you for helping get BB ready to go, I will have to thank Jake too. I feel kinda bad for laughing at him earlier." I glanced in my rearview mirror; BB was riding fine. "I've known BB since he was a baby and he still astonishes me," I said.

The drive to town didn't take too long but I still felt pressed for time. I pulled the truck into the parking lot of the old boat factory.

The factory shut down a few years ago and the parking lot had become an unofficial multi-purpose area for the county. There were periodic swap meets, farmers markets, and it had become the staging ground for the annual Christmas Parade, since there was ample room for all the floats, bands and the several horse clubs to line up without being too crowded.

"There's Zoey! Let me out here, please!" Arista reached for the door handle.

"Wait till the truck stops before bailing out, please," I said in my frustrated mom voice.

"Sorry, Mom, gotta go, Love you!" Arista shut the door and sailed off to meet her friend.

"We can unload anywhere along here." Lester pointed to an open area off to the right. "We have to get the ramps in place and roll the tractor off the trailer. We brought the ramps, didn't we, Ian?"

"Yep, we got them." Ian grinned and hopped out of the truck.

Lester and I got out of the truck. I watched them unload the tractor. BB snorted at me. I interpreted it as a question. "Not here, buddy, you and I have to go drive the truck down to the park then ride back up here." BB stomped his foot.

Once Lester and Ian had the tractor off the trailer and the ramps secured back on, I wished them luck and drove off.

I followed Main Street South, around the square and out the other side, then turned left onto Park Lane, which led over a short bridge to the Blossom Bluff City Park. Main Street allowed traffic to go in both directions, except on the square, where traffic went to the right. It can be a bit tight, particularly pulling a trailer, but I had already committed, and it would have been more complicated to turn around. When I got downtown, I realized the traffic had already been cleared in preparation for the parade. The floats were to come down Main Street, circle the Square and proceed to the park. The judges would be stationed in the Courtyard of the Square and the awards would be announced at the annual Chili Supper, held in the Blossom Bluff High School Cafeteria later in the day.

There is a bridge on Park Lane for cars and trucks to cross Spring Creek, which runs down the western edge of the park. Spring Creek is fed by Lilac Spring and Tulip Trail. A trail for pedestrians and equestrians circles the entire park and the adjacent wooded area. The town was founded in the 1800's by Reginald Lawton. His wife had his ear and a fascination with everything floral.

After finding a decent parking spot, I hopped out and dropped the tailgate for BB. "Here we are, my friend, bet you'll be glad to be out of the truck." BB snorted his agreement and jumped down. He gave his whole body a good shake for emphasis. I laughed and rubbed his neck. "You're a good mule."

I checked the saddle girth, mounted up and off we went. BB had an opinion on how we would get to Tulip Trail. I wanted to exit the parking lot on the southwest corner, but he wanted to go across the parking lot and down the well-worn path to the right of the bridge. We passed close to the dumpsters and a red and white pickup truck caught my eye. It was sitting there at a strange angle, and it was blocked in by a small black sports car.

There were three guys on the other side of the

dumpsters, two of whom I didn't recognize at all, but the third guy seemed familiar. The smaller of the two strangers raised his voice enough for me to hear. "Where's our stuff, Cabrón?"

"I don't know, I don't have it. It prolly burned up with that idiot," said the sort of familiar guy.

The little guy grabbed him by the shirt and gave him a shake. "Our boss will not like that answer, you are going to have to do better."

Familiar guy shoved back and said, "Get your filthy mitts off me, #!^%*&."

He didn't get to finish whatever he was following up with because the big guy from out of town popped him in the face with his fist. Then he mumbled something to his partner, but the only words I could make out were "El Jefe."

They looked in my direction and caught me staring. *Oh boy, this isn't good.* BB was already moving though, so I smiled and waved as if we were just passing through and hadn't been sitting there eavesdropping. Their eyes on my back made my skin crawl.

BB picked his way down the hill, jumped the creek, and proceeded up the trail in his elegant flat foot walk. I got the impression that he was quite proud of himself. I didn't know why. I nudged him up to a fox trot to put some distance between us and those weird guys.

As BB and I were nearing the intersection of Tulip Trail and 1st Avenue, I decided to cut over to the Square and pop into Cones and Scones for a coffee. While horses are not common in the city limits, they are not discouraged. Some businesses, like Sunny's Saddle Shop and Boutique, even encouraged equine patrons by providing an old-fashioned hitching post in front of their store.

We stopped at Flower Road to check for traffic before proceeding across. There was a truck barreling up the road. It appeared to be exceeding the speed limit by quite a bit. We didn't have to wait long for it to roar by, and I noticed it was the same red and white truck I had seen at the park. The guy driving looked like *Familiar Guy,* as I had taken to calling him in my head.

The truck tore past us without even slowing down. A ways up Flower Road, there is a rather sharp curve, right before the intersection with Main St.

"I hope that idiot slows down before the next intersection."

BB snorted and stamped his foot. He resumed his smooth, rhythmic flat footed walk, which is faster than a walk and not nearly as fast as his equally smooth, running walk. Speed-wise a running walk resembles a trot. We entered the Square at 1st Ave and headed for the coffee shop. Jana was leaning on her new official county-issued Ford F-150 pickup, which was parked in such a way as to block traffic from entering the Square on eastbound 1st Avenue. Jacob stood next to her, and they were chatting. They looked my way and waved. BB stopped beside them and snorted.

"Good morning! I never get tired of the sound of hooves clopping down the road." Jana patted BB's neck and slipped him a treat from her pocket.

Jana's mom made home-made animal treats and Jana kept a supply in a jar in her vehicles and a few in her pocket. Her mom's recipe involved apples, sweet potatoes and oatmeal and it was safe for multiple species.

"Good morning to you! I know, right? One of the best sounds in the world," I agreed as I dismounted. "Hey Jacob, thank you for getting BB ready to go this morning.

"No problem, sis. Do you want a Danish?" Jake pointed to a pastry box on the hood of his car and took a drink of his coffee.

"I might after I grab some coffee for myself. Can BB hang with you guys for a few minutes?"

It was a rhetorical question since BB would wait for me, and he wasn't apt to get too far away from Jana as long as she had a pocket full of snacks.

Cones and Scones was busier than usual, likely due to the impending parade and nice weather. I was eighth in line, so it was a good time to people watch, an activity Daddy and I enjoyed together from the time I was quite small. *I wish you were here today, Dad. Parade day was one of your favorites.*

The seating in Cones and Scones had recently been updated and USB outlets were added to accommodate the heightened use of electronics. There were two rows of small, raised booths down the middle of the store and a bar with stools running the length of the interior wall. A few tables were scattered in the front.

The booths were wide enough for one person to sit comfortably, the backs and the center wall of the booths were high and provided some privacy for conversation or writing the great American novel on a laptop. The line to order extended past the first two booths.

"Momma, you can't keep putting up with this, you

have got to leave him."

My ears perked up, *who said that?* I scanned the room in earnest. "Shush, someone will hear you. I know it's been bad. It will get better, he promised."

"Yeah, whatever, Mom, that is the same crap he promised last time. I mean, omg, look at your face."

I had narrowed the source of the disturbing conversation down to the booth ahead and to the left. The person directly in front of me seemed oblivious since they were playing with their phone. The line moved forward as Brandy exited the booth and we bumped into each other.

Her face turned red as she said "Sorry, Mrs. Stern, I didn't see you. I have to go."

I glanced at the person she sat with; a blonde woman had her head in her hands. I hadn't met Brandy's mom yet; they were relatively new to town. Brandy had only been to our house once or twice with Arista. The first time was a couple days before Thanksgiving and she heard about the drama, kidnapping and shooting. I wondered that night if we would ever see her again and worried what she must think of us.

I watched the woman and reached out with my intuition. *Fear, anger and shame* washed over me. *Geez, should I say something? She doesn't know me. It would come off as intrusive. I will find a way to help.*

The woman looked up then and we made eye contact. A stifling wave of embarrassment hit me, but it was coming from her. I hoped the fact I had been listening to her conversation didn't show on my face, no one enjoys being pitied. The woman gathered her handbag, tossed a dollar on the table and hurried by me.

"Please excuse me," she said so softly it was

difficult to hear.

The line moved up and I was now in second place. There was a kerfuffle behind me and a dog barked. The coffee shop was one place where dogs were not welcomed inside, but they had a very nice outdoor patio in the back, complete with fans for hot weather and propane heaters for cold weather. This was a health department rule and applied to all restaurants in the county. I peered in the direction of the noise.

The woman with the small white dog from the vet's office was near the back of the line. The dog was on a leash at her feet.

The new veterinarian, Dr. Spencer, had walked in the door. He was wearing Levi's and a dark blue Henley shirt with the sleeves pushed up. He paused for a moment, and I noticed he blinked his eyes as if adjusting from the bright sunlight outside to the more demurely lit coffee shop. That was all the time it took for the dog lady to pounce on him.

I watched her grab his arm and lean in. She said something, but I couldn't hear what it was. *Geez, poor guy, must be what a mouse feels like just before the cat lands on it.*

Dr. Spencer looked around the room and his gaze landed on me. I waved and smiled since it was the polite thing to do. It might as well have been a life raft because he pulled his arm out of the woman's grasp and spoke a little louder than necessary.

"Oh, there you are. Did you save me a spot?"

It took a beat for me to realize he was talking to me.

I saw the desperate look in his eyes and for a moment wondered if it would be more amusing to leave him hanging. A split second later I answered, "Yes I sure did save you a spot." I waved him over.

The dog lady, as I had come to think of her because I didn't know her name, gaped at me and flushed beat red. Her dog barked again and Agatha, half owner of Cones and Scones came from behind the counter and told her to please take her dog outside to the tables in back and a server would be happy to come take her order. Dog lady huffed a reply I couldn't hear and stormed out.

It was our turn to order at the counter.

Dr. Spencer pulled out his wallet. "Agatha, I'm paying for Mrs. Stern's drink order, as well as the folks behind us, since I cut the line." He handed a fifty-dollar bill to Agatha. He held a hand up in the universal *stop* sign when I began to protest.

"I appreciate the rescue. Buying you a cup of coffee is the least I can do." He grinned.

I chuckled. "How could I not? You looked like the proverbial lamb heading to slaughter, besides that woman was super rude to me in your office the other day. Who is she anyway?"

"Here ya go, doc."

Agatha slid our coffees toward us on the counter.

"Fen, here is a blueberry muffin top for BB. I remember he likes them, and I saw you ride up."

Agatha had a soft spot in her heart for all the animals that visit her shop. She only required they be well-behaved and abided by the health code. I reached for my wallet and Agatha waved me off. "Nope, BB eats on the house." She winked and turned to the next customer.

Doc had picked up our coffees and edged away from the counter towards a table. "Who is BB? Sounds like a popular guy. Husband, I guess?"

He handed me my drink. I laughed. "BB is my mule, I'm surprised you didn't see him outside waiting for me."

"The mule outside is yours? Wow, he is beautiful. I've never seen a palomino mule in person. Would you like to sit down?" Doc pointed at an empty booth.

"No thanks, I need to get going. BB and I are riding in the parade, and we need to go line up. I only stopped in for coffee."

"How will you drink it on a mule, won't it spill?" Dr. Spencer asked, looking truly puzzled.

"Nope, BB is a gaited mule, which is a bit like sitting in a rocking chair. Thanks for the coffee, doc, see ya around." I was anxious to get back outside, it was too warm inside the coffee shop for the layers I was wearing.

BB smelled the Blueberry muffin top and knickered at me to hurry up. I walked fifty feet or so over to where he stood with Jacob and Jana. "Hey buddy, Agatha sent you a muffin top, but you already know that, don't ya?" I laid the treat on the palm of my hand and held it out to my beloved mule. He ate it gently off my hand. I sipped my coffee with my other hand.

Jana turned to the side and spoke in a low voice. "So, Fen, who is the cutie that followed you out of the coffee shop? He's checking you out."

I sputtered the coffee and began to choke. Jacob smacked me on the back. "Uh, who? No, that's the new vet in town." I could feel my face flush. *Gosh it's warm out here, too.*

"Does my big sis have an admirer? Want me to talk to him?" Jacob said, grinning like a fool. He was clearly enjoying my discomfort.

"I most certainly do not. Here, hold this." I shoved my coffee cup at my bratty brother and deftly swung up into my saddle. I retrieved my coffee. "See you guys after the parade. Come on BB, we're going to be late." I glanced over at the coffee shop door and saw Dr. Spencer watching us. He waved.

I turned BB abruptly and he took off smoothly in a four-beat fox trot. As exits go, it was a good one.

CHAPTER 6

The ride up to the parade starting point was blissfully uneventful. The rhythmic clopping of BB's hooves was like a salve for my nerves. *What have I got to be nervous about? That stuff at the coffee shop and what Jana said, just plain silliness. Besides, I'm married.* My phone roared with a text message. I ignored it.

We rode into the parking lot where the floats were lined up. Our local high school marching band was warming up and getting into position and a visiting band was towards the back of the line. They looked a bit restless.

There was a troop of horses from the local saddle club behind the visiting band. The horses and any other livestock were always stationed behind the bands because sometimes they left *deposits* in the road that the band kids didn't want to march through.

BB and I headed for the group of horses, and I saw Ian and Lester on the antique tractor. They were both grinning and peering around at the other tractors, one of which appeared to be steam powered. We rode past the

FFA float, and Arista and Zoey waved and gave me the *thumbs up* sign. I smiled and waved back. It was good to see my kids enjoying themselves on such a beautiful day.

I knew most of the other riders, and we sat on our mounts and chatted until the parade Grand Marshall, Blossom Bluff Mayor, Bill Davies, announced through his megaphone the parade was about to start. Truth be told, Mayor Davies didn't really need a megaphone, he was the loudest man I had ever heard. His other job was that of an auctioneer and he had honed his voice to carry. Then we were off.

The parade spectators had filled in along the side of Main Street. They smiled and waved while the children scrambled to pick up the candy being tossed off the floats.

Twenty-five years ago, I was picking up candy along this very road, twelve years ago my Michael and I brought our twins here for their first parade. Wow, we had driven down from Kansas City in nasty weather to observe the family tradition, by the next year he was gone.

My phone roared with a text message, and I fished it out of my coat pocket. The text was from my Auntie Lou.

"Look at the past but don't live there."

How does she do that? I remembered ignoring a message notification earlier. I scrolled up. The earlier message was also from Auntie.

"Keep your eyes and ears open, things are about to get interesting. Again."

Delightful. The last time she proclaimed something like that it heralded the violent mess back in November.

Oh Goddess, I cannot go through that again.

I scanned the crowd and maneuvered BB to the outside edge of the troop of horse riders so I could see the FFA float up ahead.

There was Arista, smiling and tossing candy to the crowd, no sign of anything amiss. I twisted in my saddle to check on Ian and Lester, they were the third tractor back after the steam-powered one. I could only tell that they were chugging along and keeping pace with the other machines.

The line of floats, bands, horses and antique tractors reached the Square and the pace slowed down so the larger entrants could navigate the turns, but also so the judges could get a good look. The line stopped completely when the float directly in front of the high school band failed to negotiate the right turn and nearly wiped out a fire hydrant. To their credit, the band kept playing for a good ten minutes, standing there, not marching. Some of the horses in our group were getting restless and began to fidget. BB stood, mostly statue-like. "You are such a good mule." I patted his neck.

I entertained myself by watching people. It occurred to me to notice the architecture of the buildings on the Square. The bones were the same but there had been updates to the facades as the primary occupants and uses changed over the years.

For example, the old dime store, a two-story structure located on the south side of the Square had closed before I was born and had been an empty shell for most of my life. Now it was completely refurbished into a gym and Yvonne told me the new owner turned the upstairs into *swanky apartments*. So far. I was unable to determine what made an apartment *swanky* in the eyes of a 75-year-old.

The front window of the gym was decorated with pictures of Santa and the Grinch doing different exercises. In one scene they were in a boxing ring. Lights framed the entire window. It was cute.

My eyes traveled up the building. Standing on the balcony outside one of the *swanky* apartments was none other than Dr. Spencer. *Wow, he has a bird's eye view of the parade.* He appeared to be eating a sandwich, saw me and waved. I waved back automatically and felt my face flush. I quickly looked at the ground and dismounted. I decided to check BB's hooves for something to do.

I finished inspecting all four feet and straightened up from being bent over when I heard,

"Is your mule alright? Do you want me to take a look?"

I turned and nearly bumped into Dr. Spencer, who had come up behind me and was pointing at BB's feet. "No, everything is fine, Doc, thanks for asking. I got bored sitting here and thought to do something useful. Oh look, we are moving again!" I grinned and swung up on my mule's back.

Dr. Spencer stepped in front of BB. "You don't like me much do you, Mrs. Stern?"

BB took the hint from the leg signal I had given him. He backed up and side passed over a few steps. "I don't know why you'd think that, Doc, I just don't know you. Gotta go, see you later." BB snorted and walked on with the rest of the horses.

BB and I arrived at our truck and trailer, we would have to wait for Ian and Lester to finish the parade route and load the tractor. I poured some water in a dish for BB and got him a handful of snacks. I decided to sit in the truck and read my kindle app. It was better than worrying about my aunt's cryptic text messages or trying to figure out what Doc was talking about.

Diving into a fun book being an excellent distraction, I lost all track of time. I was so focused on the story when Ian popped up in the driver's side window and spoke, my heart landed somewhere near my tonsils.

"Hi, Mom! Dang that was fun, I love that tractor!"

Lester was a bit more reserved but was none the less grinning like a kid in a candy store. "It was fun Fen, did you see us? It ran the whole way, didn't die one time! I think we overcame the issue with the carburetor."

I quickly bookmarked my kindle and closed the app. "That's great, guys! I could only catch glimpses of y'all along the parade route, but it did appear you were having fun. Ian, have you seen your sister?"

"Yep, she was riding the float back to the high school, it will be parked there." Ian retrieved the ramps from the trailer and set them up to load the tractor.

I got out of the truck and gave BB some more water. He waited patiently near the edge of the parking lot, nibbling on grass.

"Oh hi, I don't think we've met." I offered a handshake to the man who stood next to Lester. He was an older man, older than Lester, judging by the wrinkles and age spots on his face and hands. Dressed in bib overalls, a flannel shirt and a dark brown fedora style hat. He was trim and wiry white hair stuck out from under the hat. His hazel eyes were sharp.

"Oh, we have met, you were no bigger than a minute." He gestured with his hand towards the ground. "Your daddy brung you out to my place once, my Annie fussed over you and fed you full of her ginger cookies. I don't get to town much."

"Oh, it's nice to meet you as an adult, I like your hat." I felt a bit awkward.

"It's my 'goin to town hat.' That's a fine mule." He pointed at BB. "Will he pull a plow?"

"Thanks, he never has, but I suppose he could pull a plow," I said. The old guy grunted and just like that our conversation was over.

Lester said, "Sorry Fen, I should have introduced y'all. This old coot is Ernie Montgomery. He was the one driving the steam-powered tractor today."

Ian piped up and added, "Yeah, Mom, it was way cool. Burn wood to boil the water that makes the engine go. It even has a bale spike on the back that works on pullies with a hand crank!" He fired up our tractor.

Lester went to help line it up with the ramps.

"Mr. Montgomery, your tractor made quite an impression on my son." I smiled. "I'd enjoy hearing more about it, where is it?"

"The dad-burned thing ran out of fire while we were sittin' dead in the square waitin' for that pinhead to unstick himself from the turn. I had to coast into that parking lot right off the Square and there it will set till I can get back up here with some firewood. Lester said he reckoned I could get a lift back to my truck from you'uns."

"How frustrating that must have been for you. Of course we'll be happy to give you a lift back to your truck." I suppressed a smile.

I could tell Mr. Montgomery was not amused by the delay and extra work caused by the stuck float, but his diatribe amused me.

A few minutes later Lester announced the tractor was strapped down and ready to go. I patted BB's neck and said, "You ready to load up?"

BB walked over to the tailgate of my truck and hopped in.

Mr. Montgomery took off his hat and scratched his head. "Well, I'll be dipped and rolled, what a mule."

We drove back over to the old boat factory parking lot to drop Mr. Montgomery off at his truck. Ian had asked him if he needed any help with his tractor and he declined.

"Will we see you at the chili supper after a while?" I asked.

"No, I'm wantin' to be home to my holler before dark. I thank you for the lift. Lester, you're welcome out to the house anytime, bring this here boy."

We watched as Mr. Montgomery trudged over to his truck, a ¾ ton Chevy flatbed with side rails and a gooseneck flat trailer hooked to it. There was a stack of firewood on the truck bed, up against the cab. The trailer was heavy duty and had the built on, fold down ramp.

"Whoa, that is a nice trailer! No wonder he didn't need help loading his tractor," Ian exclaimed.

Lester agreed enthusiastically.

They continued to converse about the pros and cons

of steam power versus gasoline, the absolute coolness of dovetail trailers, and I stopped listening to get lost in my own thoughts.

A text had come in from Arista asking if she could ride home with Zoey and meet us at the chili supper later. I had agreed so we were heading home to drop off the tractor, trailer, get BB settled for the night and pick up my crockpot full of chili.

I wonder if Dr. Spencer will be at the chili supper? Was I rude to him earlier? Damn, I might have been. Oh Fen, for heaven's sake what difference does it make. He is kinda cute.

"Earth to Mom!"

I felt a tap on my shoulder.

"Are you okay, Mom?"

Ian and Lester stared at me when I looked over to the passenger side of the vehicle. "Sure, why would you think otherwise?"

"You are doing that thing you do when you are worried, kind of like chewing on your lower lip. Arista says it's one of your *tells* and that you do it before you try to bluff when we are playing a game."

"Is that right, hmm," I said.

"I don't think Arista wanted you to tell her that,"

Lester whispered to Ian, even as he winked at me.

I parked the truck and we got out. The guys went to work getting the tractor unloaded, and I let BB out of the truck bed. He walked over to the barn door and waited to be let in. Once he was unsaddled, brushed and fed, I headed to the house.

The chili simmered on the lowest setting and smelled wonderful. It was my daddy's recipe, and the secret was in the homegrown peppers.

The kittens had gotten free of Arista's room and met me in the kitchen. Evidence suggested that they had gotten bored and hungry, although their attempts to bust into the cabinet where the kibble is kept were unsuccessful. I got their food ready and deposited them in the laundry room after I cuddled each kitten in turn. *I need to start trying to find suitable homes for them. Maybe Doc will know someone.*

I had a few minutes before we had to leave so I tore into my closet and found a dark green top, tunic length with ¾ length bell sleeves. I grabbed my silver charm belt, a chain belt of my own creation with an assortment of charms, some made by me and some gifted from loved ones, and clipped it around my waist. A three minute make-up refresher and rose quartz earrings with little silver dangles completed my look.

Lester and Ian were standing around in the kitchen when I entered. "Wow Mom, you look nice."

"Yeah Fen, you clean up pretty well." Lester nodded appreciatively.

"Thanks guys." *Geez I must not look that great the rest of the time, maybe I could stand to spend a bit more time on my appearance.* "Ian, will you carry the crockpot out to the truck? Do keep it level."

We loaded up in the truck and off we went to the school. Arista and her friend Zoey met us in the parking lot upon our arrival. The girls were bouncing on their heels. I thought they were excited for the upcoming event and must have some good stories to tell me about the parade. I couldn't have been more wrong. The source of their disquietude was much different.

"Moooom, you have to come quick, something has happened, and we can't find Brandy!" Arista was wringing her hands.

She never wrings her hands; this could be bad.

CHAPTER 7

"What has happened and where was Brandy supposed to meet you?" I asked, not ready to commit to a wild goose chase if this was banal teenage drama. I motioned for Ian to get the crockpot and run it into the school. "Remember to plug it in. I will be there in a moment," I called after him.

"A few minutes ago there were a bunch of sirens heading for the Square. She was supposed to meet us here. We even looked inside, and she isn't anywhere and won't answer her phone." Arista spewed this explanation so rapidly it was a bit like listening to an auctioneer.

"Okay, honey, I hear you. Maybe her phone is dead and she will be along any moment. If we leave here and go looking for her, she won't be able to find y'all when she shows up here," I said in my most reasonable mom voice.

Arista stopped bouncing and crossed her arms. *Here we go.*

"But MOM, what about the sirens? What if she got

hurt and no one knows?"

Zoey nodded along but hadn't added anything beyond, "Yeah."

"Someone knows something, that is what the sirens mean." I mirrored her stance. My daughter comes by her stubbornness honestly. We stared at each other for a moment. My intuition was waking up and the very thought of sirens piqued my curiosity. *Dang it.*

"Here is what's going to happen," I said with certainty. "You both will wait here in case Brandy shows up." I held up my hand in the classic stop motion to forestall the argument that was brewing. "I will drive over to the Square and investigate to put your minds at ease. If there is anything wrong, I'll call you."

Arista, having accepted this was the best deal she would get, uncrossed her arms with a huff. "Fine."

To Zoey's credit she put her hand on Arista's shoulder. "Thank you, Mrs. Stern, we appreciate it."

Arista said softly, "Yes, thanks, Mom. I'm just worried."

I hugged them both. "I'm sure she is fine, now go inside and make sure your brother plugged in the crockpot and that it is set up properly. I'll be back shortly."

I drove down Main Street and into the Square. Jacob's car was parked directly ahead in front of Sunny's Saddle Shop and Boutique. I had to drive around the Square because of the one-way street. My intention was to park next to Jake's car and see if he had any information or if he happened to have seen

Brandy. As I began my second left turn, I noticed flashing lights in my right-side mirror, past the Square and off to the right. I hurried to park the truck and hopped out. Something felt off.

I started towards the area of concern and jay-walked to the diagonal corner. The festive mood that permeated the Square a couple hours ago was gone, replaced by a dark, foreboding vibe that caused me to hold my breath.

I ran down the sidewalk and, when I passed the building, I stopped. The scene in the parking lot, although visible, was simply too much to take in. I saw Jacob running towards me.

The sheriff's Ford Interceptor SUV was in the parking lot with the light bar undulating minus the siren. Sheriff John Peters spoke with EMTs, Kim Edwards and Jess Falon. Deputy Jana Smith stood about 50 feet away with Brandy.

There she is, thank the Goddess. I barely had time to register that thought because the county coroner's hearse pulled in and my eyes shifted to the body dangling from the hay spike on the back of the steam powered tractor.

Jacob had me by the shoulders and shook me gently.

"Sis, are you okay? Let's get you up."

Up? I noticed cold seeping up through my rear. *I'm on the ground, how'd I get down here?*

I allowed my brother to help me to my feet. "What happened? Who is dead?" There was no way that poor person impaled on the steel spike was alive, you didn't have to be a medical examiner to know that. I shook off my revulsion.

"Not sure what happened, Jana got off duty and we decided to stop by Sunny's Boutique, but before we went inside, we heard a scream. Of course, Jana ran towards the sound to check it out. We found Brandy over there and saw the body."

Jacob wrapped a protective arm around my shoulders. "Is she alright? You haven't told me who that is?" I pointed to the body.

"I don't know who it is. Jana checked to see if there was a pulse, there wasn't. She wouldn't let anyone else near it until the sheriff got here. Brandy is understandably shaken up but is not injured that I could tell."

I walked toward Brandy and Jana, purposefully keeping my eyes off the gruesome body and the pool of blood underneath it.

"Whoa, Fen, you sort of fainted, slow down, sis."

I shook Jake's hand off my arm. "I'm fine, stunned for a minute. Don't fret, baby brother."

When I reached Jana and Brandy, Brandy looked at me with red-rimmed eyes and nearly tackled me in a hug. Fresh tears erupted and her whole body heaved with labored sobs. Jana looked sadly at the girl and patted me on the back. "I'm going to check in with the sheriff if you've got this." She motioned at the sobbing girl. I nodded an affirmative.

"Jacob, please make a run to the coffee shop, get a couple cups of Agatha's Savage Soother tea and bring them back." My brother was hovering and needed something to do. I needed to focus on Brandy, and Jana was in full on official police mode. Jake didn't look super happy about being sent away but he went.

I held Brandy while she sobbed, rocking slightly back and forth, I think it is a *mom thing*. A protective chant I learned sitting on my Auntie Louisa's lap when

I was a child flooded into my head. I began to repeat it silently.

Three Ladies came from the East
Pushing Calm before them.
One said, Out Fear,
The Second said, In Peace,
The Third said, All is Calm

After a few moments of silent chanting, Brandy's sobs began to lessen into hiccupping whimpers. I took the opportunity to survey the scene. The coroner was directing the EMTs and a couple of volunteer firemen on how to free the corpse from the spike. *When did the firemen get here? Don't remember seeing them.* The process was much too grisly to watch so I turned my attention to the rest of the parking lot. The red and white truck I had seen earlier in the day was parked at an odd angle over by the building, its nose pointed at the tractor. There were no other vehicles in the lot. Jana was taking photographs of the scene and Sheriff Peters was on his phone. Try as I might, I was unable to hear what he was saying.

Jacob came back with the tea, and he had a small blanket draped over his arm.

"Here honey, drink this." I patted Brandy's back and stepped away as Jacob handed one of the cups to her and the other to me. He then placed the blanket around Brandy's shoulders and stepped between her and the sight of the body on the spike. My brother isn't a large man, tall yes, at about 6'2" but not overly wide. I hoped he would take up enough space to block her view, should she look in that direction. I moved a bit to my left, and she instinctively turned towards me. *Good girl.*

She took a sip of the hot tea and made to look over her shoulder at the recovery activities.

The coroner had shouted, "Careful now, don't pull, go straight up."

"Sorry doc, this is a big guy, he's heavy," said one of the firemen.

Brandy whimpered when she heard that, and I worried the uncontrolled tears would start again so I silently resumed my chant. Jacob was watching me closely. *I wonder if he can tell I'm chanting in my head?*

Jacob received much of the same training in the arcane arts as I did, also from Auntie Lou, and I knew he could work some basic healing spells but his acumen always leaned towards working for Prosperity and Success. Our mother, who for whatever reason, was unable to work any spell or chant was very artistic. She taught Jacob to paint the Pennsylvania Dutch Hex Signs, the colorful ones most often seen on barns.

They are ubiquitous throughout Pennsylvania, Ohio and parts of Appalachia but can be seen anywhere there is a history of primarily German immigrants if you know what you are looking for. There are several dozen barns in our county adorned with the colorful, historic signs, including ours.

"Sheriff, can you call for some more guys to give us a hand?" shouted one of the firemen.

"Can't you lower the spike a bit? Looks like it is on a pully type hoist thing." Jana pointed at the crank.

"Ah, yes, good idea. You are one smart cookie, deputy." The coroner nodded.

"Thanks, Doc, wear gloves though, the crime team

will probably want prints from it," Jana said snapping some more photos of the position of the hand crank and the angle of the spike.

I tuned it all out and refocused on Brandy, who, thankfully, was drinking her tea and looking less pale. "Jacob, will you please check with Sheriff Peters and get permission to take Brandy away from here?"

Jake nodded and left but he was back moments later with an *okay* from the sheriff. "I'm gonna run my car keys over to Jana. We already dropped her rig at the station. I'll be right back."

"Brandy, where is your momma right now?" I asked.

"She's at work at the nursing home. Oh God, she doesn't know yet, I have to get there." She started to shake.

Sheriff Peters walked over to us, and he overheard us talking about Brandy's mom. His eyes read kindness, and I had known him since I was little, so I saw the wheels turning in his mind. I was sure that we were wondering the same thing: *Who was this man to her and her mother?*

"Brandy, honey, who is the man over there? He's not your dad, is he?" I asked softly.

Brandy replied, "God no, he is my mom's boyfriend." A fire flashed briefly in her eyes and the last word was laced with contempt. I glanced at Sheriff Peters, he had noticed it too.

"Brandy, can you tell me the man's name?" asked the sheriff.

"It's Darren, Darren McNamara. I'm surprised you don't know him, he was always talking about being from here, like he invented the place."

"How old are you, Brandy?" asked the sheriff.

"Fifteen, sir. I'll be sixteen in March."

I watched enough cop shows to know what the sheriff was thinking. *The victim is known to this young woman and her mother. The sheriff will want to be the one to notify the mother so he can evaluate her reaction to the news. Brandy is a minor and must have a parent or guardian present if detailed questioning is done by law enforcement.*

"Brandy, I need you to go with Mrs. Stern for now. I will go straight over and let your mom know what happened." Sheriff Peters spoke in a soft baritone voice laced with authority.

Brandy gave a faint nod and pulled the blanket tighter around her shoulders. The warmth we'd enjoyed earlier in the day faded the moment the sun went down.

"Jacob, will you please escort Brandy up to my truck? Here are the keys, show her how to turn the seat heater on, and I will be there in a minute."

He looked quizzically back at me, but he accepted the keys, and I motioned subtly to the sheriff. "Sure thing, sis." Jacob turned to Brandy and said, "Come on Brandy, you look cold and Fen's heated seats are the bomb."

Once Jake and Brandy had walked about thirty feet away, I asked the sheriff, "So do you know Darren McNamara? I feel like I've heard the name, but I can't place him."

Sheriff Peters grimaced. "Yep, I know the name. Every cop in four counties knows his name. The guy was always like Teflon, nothing ever stuck to him. Till now. I'm not surprised you don't know him, y'all didn't run in the same circles, Fen."

"I assume you want to be the one to tell Brandy's

mom so you can gauge her reaction. I need to tell you about a conversation I overheard this morning at the coffee shop." I repeated what I heard to Sheriff Peters, verbatim.

Jana walked over to us as I finished telling my story. The sheriff nodded. "Jana, the victim's name is Darren McNamara, and he is the boyfriend of Brandy's mother. I'm going to see her now. I know you are technically off duty, but could you stay and babysit the scene until the State Crime Technicians get here?"

"Of course, boss, no problem. The victim's name matches the registration for that red and white pickup truck." Jana pointed at the truck. "I will have the techs process it then impound it."

"That truck! I need to tell you what else I saw today!" I related the details of the altercation at the park between the victim, formerly known as *Familiar Guy*, and the two out- of -towners, then how the truck had raced past me on Flower Road. The sheriff and Deputy Jana Smith both listened intently and took notes.

My phone went crazy in my pocket, a roaring tiger notified me of an incoming text and the ringtone, Ride of the Valkyries, erupted loudly announcing a call from my daughter. *Oops, I was supposed to call her when I found Brandy.* I sighed and retrieved the phone from my pocket.

"Thank you for the information, Fen, if you think of anything else let me know." The sheriff walked toward the antique tractor.

"I will catch up with y'all later at your house," Jana said.

I clicked on my phone. "Hi honey, I found Brandy. She is okay but it's a long story. We will be up there in a short while."

Arista attempted to pepper me with questions over the phone, but I cut her off and told her she would have to wait. By this time, I had walked half the distance to my truck and checked the text messages. There were several from Arista I hadn't heard and one from Auntie Lou.

"Fen, there are too many cooks in the kitchen, don't get burned."

What? Good grief.

I was still shaking my head over that message when I got into the passenger side of the truck, content to let my brother drive.

"Where to, sis?" he asked, as he put the truck in reverse to exit the space.

"The high school. Your niece is losing her mind with worry over what we have been doing and where Brandy has been."

I turned in my seat so I could see Brandy. She was huddled in the backseat with the blanket.

"Oh yeah, I bet she's freaking out. I was supposed to meet her and Zoey like hours ago," Brandy said with a grim smile. "Your brother was right though, these heated seats are awesome." After an awkward pause she asked, "Do you think my mom is okay? I feel like I should go see her. What if she needs me?"

"I am sure your mom is fine, the sheriff is one of the kindest men I have ever known and we," I pointed between Jake and myself, "have known him all our lives. He will break the news gently and make sure she knows you are safe. If she needs anything he will bend over backwards to see that she gets it."

She watched my face, probably for signs of

dishonesty, as well as Jacob's body language. He had nodded his agreement to my description of our longtime family friend, the sheriff.

"Wow, I've never heard a cop described that way before, he must be cool," Brandy said.

I wondered why such a young person would have had a frame of reference for how any *cops* were described but I let it go and asked, "Had Mr. McNamara and your mom been dating long?"

Brandy rolled her eyes. "Too long. Look, Mrs. Stern, I know you overheard me and Mom talking in the coffee shop this morning. Darren was mean, he got mean right after we moved down here from Springfield. Before that he was sweet as pie to Mom and nice enough to me. I am not glad he's dead, but I won't miss him." Brandy stilled and stared out the window.

I couldn't think of any good way to respond so I stayed quiet and looked over at Jacob. He glanced my way with an expression that conveyed surprise and sadness.

Arista and Zoey were out in the parking lot of the school waiting for us to pull in. The truck was barely in park when Brandy slung open the door and vaulted out into the open arms of her friends. They took off for the building, probably to find an unlocked classroom to catch up without being overheard.

I heaved a sigh and looked at Jacob. "What did you make of that?"

"That we were lucky to have awesome parents that stayed together and a stable home life. Also, I truly hope this evening's events are the extent of your involvement in this mess."

Jacob looked at me in an admonishing way, as if the

trouble we all had last month was somehow avoidable. It wasn't.

Even as I agreed with him, I knew it wasn't to be.

CHAPTER 8

The festive mood inside the high school gymnasium and the smell of a dozen different pots of chili under normal circumstances would have made me happy and excited to visit with everyone and eat some great food. It was a potluck, too, and the desert table was a trip to carb heaven.

Tonight, it made me tired. I hadn't had time to process my thoughts and emotions since I had been in *supportive mother-bear* mode at the scene of the murder.

Murder, that is what it was, right? Has to be. Our tiny town used to be so quiet. If someone died from something besides sickness or old age it was probably a hunting accident or a vehicle accident like what killed daddy.

I was sitting on the steps outside the gym, procrastinating going inside. Completely lost in my own thoughts, I was startled to hear my name.

"Hi, Mrs. Stern, we keep bumping into each other."

I looked up to see Dr. Spencer smiling at me. His

smile quickly changed to a concerned grimace. It was the same look he had on his face when he examined my wayward kittens. *Great, I must look pitiful indeed.*

"Are you okay? If you're not feeling well, I can go find your husband, or I think I saw your brother inside."

I recognized *concerned doctor voice* and I bristled. "Would that you, or anyone for that matter, could find my husband. He was listed MIA in the Middle East ten years ago. As for my baby brother, he can continue trying to enjoy what is left of this wretched day. I am fine. I don't need anything."

I watched the color drain from the good doctor's face. I knew I overreacted. The stress of the last couple hours and the embarrassment of my outburst combined into a weight I wouldn't carry for much longer. *Dammit, I will not cry, not in front of this guy anyway.*

I squeezed my eyes shut to stem the tears that were threatening to spew and blinked a few times, "I'm sorry doc, that was uncalled for, the last few hours have been super stressful, please excuse me." I took off in the direction of the ladies' room, praying silently it was empty.

I burst through the door to the multi stall ladies' room, and it was, in fact, occupied. Fortunately, the girls sitting on the counter swinging their legs and chatting were Arista, Zoey and Brandy. I immediately schooled my face into neutrality. *The hot-mess-express meltdown I deserved would have to wait.* "Hey girls, I wondered where y'all went."

"Hey Mom, it was too peopley out there, so we came in here," Arista explained with a subtle glance at Brandy.

Zoey waved at me and Brandy managed a weak

smile.

Arista loves people, so does Zoey, I got it, Brandy needed some quiet. Goodness, who could blame her.

"Yeah, I feel the same way tonight. I will be relieved when we can pack it in and head home. Have you seen your grandmother? I'm sure she won't want to miss the announcement about the float contest," I said hoping for a conversation topic that wouldn't cause either Brandy or me to burst into tears.

"Grams is with Yvonne. They were hanging with some of the other old people from the Senior Center. She is super stoked about the contest and is sure their float is gonna win. Oh shoot, what time is it? I promised her we would be watching in case they win. Mayor Davies is going to announce the winners of the parade contests and the chili cookoff at 7p.m."

Zoey was the first to reach her phone and check the time. "It's 6:56, we better hurry."

As they made to leave, Brandy hugged me. "Mrs. Stern, I didn't thank you earlier for helping me. I really do appreciate it." She scurried after Arista and Zoey before I could respond.

It occurred to me I should be watching the contest announcement too. Although I wanted my family and friends to do well and have fun, I really couldn't care much about float contests now. Nevertheless, I freshened up, washed my hands, and walked out into the hallway.

Outside the double doors going to the gymnasium and along the wall I saw Dr. Spencer again. This time he was essentially cornered by the *Dog Lady*. She held her pooch like a football with one arm and had her other hand on the doc's arm. He looked rather miserable. His eyes met mine, I raised my eyebrows and shook my head. *Dude, I rescued you from her once today already, you're on your own.* I strode into the gym without a backwards glance.

The sound system screeched. "Everyone, may I please have your attention? I want to take this opportunity to thank everyone for the support at the polls last month. I am honored to be your mayor for another term. Now, without further ado, I will announce the winners of the 95th Annual Blossom Bluff Parade float contest as well as the Winner of the 23rd Annual Chili Cookoff. For those of you who may be new to our lovely community, let me relate the history behind these wonderful events."

"What happened to *without further ado?*"

A heard the whisper come from behind me. I laughed and turned to find Dr. Spencer standing with his hands in his pockets and looking a bit sheepish. "Wow, you escaped, well done."

"You could have given a guy a hand, that woman is relentless," he shuddered.

"Sorry, Doc, I reached my daily quota on number of people rescued today. If you're not one of my own kids, you are plum out of luck tonight." *OMG, am I flirting with him?* I felt my face heat so I turned back towards the stage where the mayor was still talking about the history of the Parade, the Chili cookoff and how they came to be combined on the same day. Blah Blah Blah.

"So, um, Mrs. Stern, I wanted to apologize for earlier, I didn't mean to dredge up wounds or hurt your feelings. I, uh, what I was really trying, I mean—"

He stammered a bit, appearing to be disquieted by his own word choice but unable to stop talking. *Bless his heart, that's kinda cute.*

I held up a hand to stop him. "It's fine, really. You're not from here, you couldn't have known about my loss, and on a day with less drama I wouldn't have flipped out." *Stop talking, Fen.*

"I heard something about that, a body was found, and you were there to help some girl. I also heard about some drama last month. Being new to town it's hard to separate truth from fiction, but if even half of it is true, you sure lead an interesting life."

The charming smile was back. I found myself tempted to spill my guts right there. I also wanted to find out who had been gossiping about me.

"And the winner is Blossom Bluff Senior Center with their float, theme *Frozen in Time!*"

Applause erupted throughout the gym. I swear I heard my mother whooping it up across the room. I watched as the head administrator of the Senior Center walked up on stage followed by my mother, Yvonne and another lady I couldn't name. Mom and Yvonne were co-chairs of the float committee.

I smiled. Mom was doing the Queen Wave and grinning like a kid in a candy shop, and her friend was next to her, hands clasped at chest level and bouncing on the balls of her feet. The administrator gave a short acceptance speech, and they all exited the stage to more applause. I clapped loudly and offered up a *whoohooo* of my own. I glanced at doc and exclaimed, "That's my mom!" I began to thread my way through the crowd to congratulate her.

"Hey, Momma, congratulations, you too, Yvonne!" I gave them each a hug in turn.

"Thank you, darlin', it is such an honor to win." Mom beamed.

"The best part is the $500 prize money we won will get added to the money we raised on the raffle, and it all goes to the Alzheimer's Awareness Organization!" Yvonne said, she was still bouncing.

"What raffle?"

Dr. Spencer had followed me over to my mother's table and he stood close behind me to the right. *Why is he following me? Must be trying to stay away from the Dog Lady.* I smiled inwardly at the absurdity of that.

The ladies looked Dr. Spencer over quizzically and then peered at me expectantly.

"Momma, Yvonne, this is Dr. Spencer, the veterinarian who is visiting and running the office while our Dr. Johnson is in South America. Doc, this is my mother, Marieanna Stonehorse and our friend, Yvonne Hutchins." They shook hands and exchanged pleasantries when Arista and her friends came over.

"Great job, Grams!" Arista wrapped her grandmother in a hug.

Zoey and Brandy chimed in, and I heard Yvonne launch into an explanation of the benefit raffle. To his credit, doc listened intently to Yvonne.

Huh, maybe he was genuinely curious about the raffle and not just insinuating himself into our conversation. Geez Fen, why would you think that?

The mayor ran through the second and third place winners quickly. "Now moving on to the Chili Cookoff, for the second year running, First Place goes to Fenreya Stern!"

It took a hot second for it to register. With everything that had happened, I had forgotten about my pot of chili. The whoops, whistles and loud *atta girls* from my family and closest friends were deafening. Lester pounded my back, and I heard Jacob holler.

"Oh yeah, that's my sis!"

My stars! Someone propelled me towards the steps leading to the stage, I'm pretty sure it was Arista. I froze at the bottom of the steps. Ian offered me his arm and escorted me up the stairs.

My son is a gentleman, I'm not completely sure how it happened but I knew it was not completely my doing.

I walked to the podium and shook the mayor's proffered hand. He nodded encouragingly at me as I looked out upon the audience. I saw the *Dog Lady* looking daggers at me.

Something about that lit a fire deep inside me. I smiled directly at her and then around the gym. I spoke into the microphone, "Thank you, Blossom Bluff, the best little town in Missouri! I'm donating my prize to the Free Spay and Neuter program." I turned to exit. I was ever so grateful for Ian's arm going down the steps, it would have been a real bummer to fall.

Amid more hugs and congratulations, I heard the mayor.

"Second place goes to newcomer to town and the new Superintendent of Schools, Miss Marcia Vanderkamp!" There was mild applause and a few murmurs from people wondering who the newcomer was, and if she was there.

I was standing in the middle of my people and I asked, "Who is that?"

Ian pointed and I followed his finger, even as I put

my hand on his arm and pushed it down. "Don't point, honey, it's rude." Then I saw the *Dog Lady* looking red faced but smiling and doing the Princess Wave. *You have got to be kidding me.*

Brandy said, "Oh my mom just texted me; she is outside waiting for me. I gotta go!" She promised to call Arista and Zoey later, waved bye and rushed out.

"Congratulations on your win, Mrs. Stern, and that was pretty cool, donating your cash prize to the Free Spay/Neuter Program." Dr. Spencer grinned.

"Thanks, Doc, how about you call me Fen from now on?" I smiled up at him.

"Okay, then you should call me Will."

There was a crash over by the food tables. "Oh my goodness, look at that!" Dog Lady said loudly. *Shoot, what was her name? Marcia something. Who am I kidding, she was always going to be Dog Lady in my head.* I walked over to investigate the commotion.

My crockpot lay on the floor, the ceramic pot part was broken. Prize winning chili spilled out onto the floor.

"Oh dear, was that yours? I am so sorry. I tripped and next thing I knew it toppled right off the table!" Dog Lady spoke louder than necessary.

Yeah right, you look about as sorry as the cat who ate the canary. "No worries, it was an old crock, and I've got another full pot of chili at home. I hope it doesn't stain your pretty gym floor." I put the emphasis on *your* since she was the school superintendent. I figured the upkeep and repairs to school property were in her wheelhouse. Most definitely wasn't my problem.

Arista shot the woman a dirty look as she stooped to pick up the electric part of the appliance and the lid, which was remarkably unbroken. A couple kids on the clean-up committee stepped in to rectify the rest of the mess.

My mother ambled over, took a look at the mess, the Dog Lady and then commented, "She's a bit clumsy, eh? I'm tired. Yvonne is driving me home to watch Gibbs, then I'm going to bed. Might sleep for a week."

"Okay, Momma, goodnight. We will be along shortly. Yvonne, you are welcome to stay at the house if you want to." Yvonne was Mom's oldest friend, she frequently stayed over so they could get an early start in the morning. They ran around doing various volunteer work and fun events at the Senior Center, in fact I worried sometimes Momma was wearing herself out. They were busier than some people who work for a living. Both ladies seemed to love it though, and Yvonne has been worth her weight in gold. Ever since Mom was diagnosed with Alzheimer's she doesn't drive anymore. Nor does she cook or spend long periods of time alone.

"I think I will Fen, thank you. I am mighty tired."

Yvonne ushered Mom toward the door.

"Arista, round up your brother and Lester please, and tell them to meet me at the truck, it's time to go. Is Zoey riding with us? Oh, and please put the crockpot in the bed of the truck."

"Yes, if that's okay, yeah I will find them." Arista left with the remains of the crockpot. Zoey trailed along with her, carrying their jackets and handbags.

Ian jogged over, his two best friends, Tom and JJ

were with him. "Hey, Mom, is it okay if the boys come home with us?"

"Of course, as long as their folks know where they are. It's going to be a tight fit in the truck though."

"Tom's got his car, it's tiny but the three of us can jam in there," Ian said.

Tom, being a few months older than my kids, already had his driver's license and he got a *new to him* Volkswagen Beetle, and the thought of three lanky teenage boys threading themselves into it amused me. I suppressed a giggle; Tom was proud of his car, and I wouldn't hurt his feelings for anything. "Okay, Tom, drive safe. Ian and JJ don't distract him while he's driving. Will you be going straight home?"

There was a chorus of "Yes, ma'ams."

I noticed the *Dog Lady* watching us with a scowl on her face. *Geez, what is her problem? The new Superintendent of the school hates me. I hope she doesn't take it out on my kids and their friends.*

I turned my attention back to Dr. Spencer, who seemed to be waiting around for something. "It was nice talking to you, Doc, have a good night."

He smiled, "I thought you were going to call me Will." He chuckled. "Can I walk you out?"

I glanced at the *Dog Lady* who watched Will like a hawk watches a rabbit, and I decided having a handsome doctor escort me out to my truck was a jolly idea. "Thank you, Will, that would be lovely."

CHAPTER 9

When I got home with Arista, Zoey, Jacob, and Lester, the lights were on in the kitchen. I noticed Yvonne's car in the driveway but no sign of Tom's VW Bug. *Oh dear, I hope the boys didn't have trouble of some kind.*

I made some coffee for Lester and me. The girls were playing with the kittens. Jana drove up in Jacob's car and came inside. She looked exhausted and gratefully accepted the cup of coffee I put in front of her. Jacob gave her a one-armed hug as she settled on a stool at the kitchen island.

"You missed the chili supper, are you hungry?" I asked my friend.

"I could eat. Geez, what a craptastic day this has been!" Jana shook her head.

I heated up some chili on the stove and got some grilled cheese sandwiches going. Those boys would be hungry again when they got home, might as well get prepared.

A few moments later the kitchen door opened and

the room filled with exuberant teenage boy energy and a jumble of talking.

"Yeah, I wonder what happened to old man Montgomery?"

"Two busted tires on that big ole trailer sucks, dude."

"Dude, they weren't busted, they were cut. Oh, grilled cheese!"

Jana, Jacob, Lester and I perked up and stared at the boys. Lester spoke first.

"What do you mean what happened to Montgomery? What trailer?"

"We cruised by the old boat factory lot and his trailer was still sitting there, no sign of him or his truck. The trailer has two slashed tires," Ian said and grabbed a grilled cheese.

"Y'all stopped there to do donuts in the parking lot, didn't ya?" I asked, narrowed eyes peering at each of the boys. It wasn't really a question, there was only one reason teenage boys visited an empty parking lot at night in a fun little car.

"Well, um," Tom mumbled down at his feet.

He didn't meet my eyes.

"Yes, ma'am." JJ was also looking at the floor.

Bless him, JJ always told the truth.

Ian and Tom glared at JJ. "Dude!"

"What? We were already blown. Besides someone needs to check on the old guy," JJ said.

Jana had her cop face back on. "Tell me exactly what you saw."

The boys took turns telling the story in between bites of grilled cheese. Arista and Zoey sauntered in, each held a kitten.

Basically, they pulled into the parking lot at the old boat factory. The lot was empty, save for Mr. Montgomery's trailer.

Ian thought it was strange for it to still be sitting there, but he knew the antique steam-powered tractor, belonging to Mr. Montgomery, had become an active crime scene and had been impounded by the sheriff. The slashed tires were most worrisome.

The little yellow and white kitten stopped scurrying around the kitchen and mewed. I picked him up absently and cuddled him to my chest. "Gosh, I hope Mr. Montgomery is all right. Lester. do you have his phone number? We should check on him."

"If he has a phone at his house, I don't know the number." Lester shook his head.

"Can't we text him?" Zoey asked.

Lester laughed. "That old codger doesn't believe in cell phones, thinks the government uses them to spy on people." This drew horrified looks from every teenager in the room. "And it's too late at night to drive over to his place, apt to be met by buckshot, best wait till morning."

Jana excused herself to go call the sheriff and report this new development.

"Tomorrow is Sunday, how about Lester and I run out to the Montgomery place and see what's up?" The bitty cat wriggled in my arms trying to get to my earring.

Lester downed the last of his coffee. "That works for me. I'm gonna turn in now so we can go early in the morning. About seven a.m. work for you, Fen?"

I usually sleep in on Sundays and I secretly wished I'd kept my mouth shut, but instead I smiled and said,

"Sure, sounds like a plan."

Jana returned to the kitchen and sighed, "The sheriff says he will meet me out at the lot where the trailer is tonight. We'll take a look and grab some pictures. He's going to see if he can locate a land line phone number for Montgomery. Jacob, would you mind driving me over there? I can get a lift home from the sheriff if you don't want to wait."

Jacob grinned at Jana. "I will take you anywhere you want to go day or night, darlin'," then he winked at her.

She's blushing! They are both smitten.

"You two are adorable." I handed the naughty kitten off to Arista. "Here honey, take this wee beastie and keep him out of trouble. I'm going to bed, evidently tomorrow is going to start early."

I grabbed a quick shower and went to bed. My mind churned through the day's events, and I could not find a comfortable position. After an hour of tossing about and rehashing the day, I gave up and got back up. Insomnia was not a common issue for me but when it happened there's only one thing that works.

I grabbed my earbuds and headed downstairs quietly. I doubted the kids were actually asleep, but they had gone to their respective rooms and everyone else would be asleep.

Downstairs is divided into three spaces. Along one side to the right of the stairs there are two large chest freezers, a large countertop sits perpendicular to them. An oversized stainless-steel sink and a gas range top completes the area. There are shelves under the counter where we keep the bulk of canned goods from the garden. To the left of the stairs is a spare bedroom which rarely gets used and my jewelry studio. I love my studio, it is full of natural light from the South facing windows and I can spend hours in there puttering with my jewelry tools. The remaining part of the downstairs is an open floorplan, set up like a gym.

I headed to the gym. There, I had my choice of an elliptical machine, some free weights, floor space for yoga and a heavy punching bag suspended from the ceiling.

I met my husband, Michael, at college. It was a chance meeting, he heard me getting attacked and came to my rescue. We began hanging out as friends. I had been shaken up by the attack and had no interest in dating anyone at the time. Michael was a blackbelt in Taekwondo and Krav Maga and he taught me how to use Krav Maga techniques to defend myself. The training has come in handy more times than I like to think about over the years.

I took a moment to put on gloves, having raw knuckles from wailing on the bag was never my idea of a good time.

I was scared. I was angry about feeling scared. The trouble was I couldn't completely identify what was causing the emotion of fear.

Seeing the man impaled on the bale spike was scary. Random violence around my community in the form of abused animals, beaten dogs, burning motor homes and slashed tires was unsettling to be sure.

I hammered on the bag. There was more to it. *What is wrong with me?* The voice inside my head, the one I associate with my grandmother said, "Baby girl, look forward, move forward."

NO, I can't.

"You must, a tree that doesn't spread its roots and

branches, doesn't participate in the cycle, dies."

I hugged the bag and sank to my knees on the floor. Unstoppable tears rolled down my face as I melted all the way to the floor, and I sobbed.

I'm not sure how long I stayed there, crumpled and crying. Something touched my hair. *Mew?* It sounded like a question. The something touched my hair again and there was a small rumbling noise. I pushed myself up and found myself face to tiny face with the yellow and white kitten.

"How did you get here?" I sat back on my knees and wiped my tears on my t-shirt.

The kitten sat like a statue, staring up at me. "Mew."

I thought about my thoughts and decided to set them aside for the rest of the night. My body finally felt relaxed, and my emotions were no longer boiling. I picked up the kitten. "Sometimes a good old-fashioned hissy fit is all it takes, huh Punkin?"

"Mew!"

As I walked upstairs, I puzzled over what to do with kitty. I didn't want to wake the girls by opening Arista's door to put him in there, but I couldn't bear to lock him in the laundry room by himself. "You're coming with me kitty, let's go get some sleep." This was met with purring.

Isabella, the self-appointed feline queen of house, was not delighted to see the upstart kitten join us in bed. Although, to her credit she glared at us and went back to sleep. I turned the light out and the last thing I felt before drifting off was tiny paws in my hair.

CHAPTER 10

The alarm feature on my phone blared at six a.m. I rolled over and silenced it. Ten minutes later it went off again. *It's Sunday, why the hell, oh yeah. Dang it.* I opened my eyes and peered around.

When I tried to rise, my hair was held down, and I turned to see what it was caught on. Two bright blue eyes blinked at me, followed by the biggest yawn a tiny creature could manage. "Good morning, Little Bit." I gently dislodged the kitty from my hair and got up.

There was no reason to get all fixed up to run the errand Lester and I planned, but I dislike leaving the house without at least brushing my teeth and making sure my hair didn't look like something had built a nest in it. Last night something had. The mirror further informed me that my eyes were puffy, and my face was chapped. Salty tears are apparently kind of tough on skin.

Great, if I go out there looking like this, everyone in the house will wonder what is wrong. I washed my face with the coldest water I could stand, followed with a hot washcloth, and quickly applied moisturizer. *A little makeup won't hurt.* I brushed my hair and put it in a messy bun, donned jeans, boots and a light blue Henley and headed for the kitchen.

Lester had the coffee ready and was eating an English muffin with homemade apple butter on it. "Good morning, Fen, how did you sleep?"

Oh no, did he overhear my crying fit? Did everyone else? Just be cool. "Fine as frog's hair, how about you?" It wasn't a lie, I did sleep well after I finally got to sleep.

"I always sleep well, except little Violet woke up and barked a couple times. I hope she didn't wake anyone else," he said.

"I never heard her." I breathed a silent sigh of relief. "Thank you for making coffee. I'm ready to go whenever you are, no rush though."

Lester finished his breakfast, and I wrote a note to leave for Yvonne. The kids might or might not be up when we returned from our errand. When I grabbed my handbag off the back of the kitchen chair, it was heavier than normal. A tiny white head with a yellow spot popped up from inside. "Oh, my stars, how did you get in there?" I plucked the kitten out of my bag and carried him down the hall to Arista's room. I eased the door open and deposited the kitten inside. "Mrow!"

"Shoosh, you can't go with me." I closed the door.

The drive out to the Montgomery farm was uneventful except for the fog. We drove slowly and sipped our to-go cups of coffee. Lester broke the silence after a few miles, "What do you make of that killin'?"

"Jeepers, what an awful thing. I'd like to think it was a freak accident, but the sheriff doesn't seem to think so, and if I'm being honest, I cannot conceive of how it could accidently happen. Did you know the guy, Darren McNamara?"

Lester sipped his coffee, "Only by name and reputation. He was not known for being a nice man. Have you heard if they figured out who burned up in that motor home fire?"

"Not yet, if Jana knows, she hasn't mentioned it." I hit my brakes when a skunk ambled across the road without a care in the world.

"Phew, glad you missed 'im. In about a mile you'll want to turn left, it's a dirt road," Lester said.

I followed Lester's directions. The dirt road wasn't terrible but the next one we turned down to the right was native rock and clay. It didn't appear to have seen a grader in my lifetime. We bounced along forever and finally a homestead appeared. Tidy house and yard framed by a rail fence, the adjacent machine shed was chock full of old equipment and random pieces of metal. There was a barn about 75 feet from the machine shed and several cows and a handful of goats stood around munching hay. There were chickens everywhere. There was another little building, barely visible from the driveway, behind the house. Smoke puffed out of a metal chimney. It was larger than any smokehouse I had ever seen, not that I had seen that many, they had mostly been retired in favor of the little barrel smokers on wheels from the big box stores.

"Lester, what kind of little building is that?" I asked pointing. Lester pushed my pointing finger down.

"Don't ask."

We got out of the truck and several dogs ran out from under the porch to greet us. None of them acted mean, but they were very interested in investigating us. A bloodhound on the porch sat up and bayed loudly.

"That there is what we call an Ozark Alarm System. I think Mick will know we're here now." Lester chuckled.

"You've been here before, haven't you?" I eyed Lester and thought of the little flask he kept squirreled away in his bib overalls pocket. A few tidbits of information came together.

Before he could think of an answer, the front door of the house opened and Mr. Montgomery poked his head out the door. "What's your business on a Sunday morning clear out here?"

"Morning, Mick, we've come to check on ya. The kids seen your trailer downtown with slashed tires and we're jus' makin' sure you're okay," Lester explained.

It appeared Mr. Montgomery set something down inside the house and came out onto the porch. *Geez, I bet that was a shotgun. I think we drove through a wormhole and into the 1940s.*

Mr. Montgomery peered at us and ran a hand over his head.

"Hrumpf, I suppose y'all should come in and have some coffee then. You come as a kindness and my Annie would roll over in her grave if I didn't offer you some hospitality."

The sea of dogs parted, and we made our way to the three steps leading up onto the porch. The bloodhound stood up, stretched and came over for the obligatory sniff. Evidently satisfied with what he smelled, he nudged my hand up to pet his head.

Bloodhounds naturally have kind of a musky scent. I've never thought of it as anything but distinctive but my favorite thing about a bloodhound is their marvelous ears, they remind me of velvet.

Mr. Montgomery ushered us into the house and the bloodhound followed. He then flopped down on the floor near the wood stove. It was boiling hot in the house, I was grateful to have left my jacket in the truck.

Mr. M proceeded to fill two cups with coffee from the percolator pot on top of the wood stove. He didn't offer cream, and I didn't ask. He then produced a flask from his pocket and poured a smidgen of the contents into his own cup, subsequently offering it to Lester and me in turn. I started to refuse but the sideways warning look Lester shot me made me acquiesce. *When in Rome...*

We all settled at the old, scarred kitchen table. *Oh if this table could talk what stories it would tell.* I watched the two older gentlemen as they sat there, silently sipping their coffee, puzzled by how information would be exchanged if no one spoke. I was about to break the silence myself when my inner *grandma* voice spoke, "Be patient, Goddess gave you two eyes and ears and only one mouth for a reason." *Patience indeed, I don't want to make a career out of this conversation.*

Lester said, "That was some parade yesterday."

Mr. Montgomery said, "Yep."

More silence. I sipped my very strong coffee and stared at the bloodhound, watching his abdomen rise and fall rhythmically as soft snores emitted from his muzzle. *Lucky dog, I could still be in bed.*

Mr. Montgomery began, "I met my Annie at that

parade many years ago. My folks didn't bring us kids to town but twice a year. Once was to the Christmas Parade. We always looked forward to it because of the store-bought candy. One year, when I was about thirteen, I reached to pick up a piece of candy on the street and the prettiest little girl I ever seen reached for the same piece. I had snatched the candy off the ground, but I took one look at her big blue eyes, and I was done. I gave her the candy. She giggled and ran off.

"I didn't see her again until the next year's parade. I was ready then, I found her, gave her a whole handful of candy and asked her to the square dance after the parade. There weren't no chili cookoff back then, just a potluck supper and good hill music.

"We got married the next year. My Annie died three years ago August. We went to the parade every year till she couldn't travel no more. Now I go and make sure to chuck candy to the kids." Mr. Montgomery heaved a sigh and sipped his coffee.

I racked my brain to find a suitable response and realized anything I could say ran the risk of trivializing the story he'd shared. I smiled, nodded and sipped my coffee.

Lester spoke next. "So, Mick, we did come out to make sure you was okay, but we need to tell you something too."

"About my tractor? Yeah, I know. Sheriff Peters rang my phone last night and tol' me all about it. He said they'd have it for a while till they sort out what happened to that idiot. Promised he wouldn't let nothing happen to it. That sheriff's okay, for a gover'ment man." Mr. Montgomery got up to get more coffee.

I declined the refill but Lester accepted it and the flask when it came around. I tiptoed into the conversation with, "My son, Ian, was impressed by your tractor, he wanted me to ask you if you needed a hand fixing your trailer tires or retrieving your tractor once the police release it."

"He's a good boy, Fenreya Stonehorse, you done raised him well. Tomorrow I'm gonna call the tire shop down there in town and have 'em replace the tires. That sheriff wants the cut ones for evidence, don't know what good that'll do. The pinhead that cut 'em is dead, ain't like he would've paid for them anyhow."

"Do you mean to say that Darren McNamara is the one that cut your tires? Are you sure?" I asked, my wheels turning now. *If the dead guy cut Mick's tires, then wouldn't it be a possible motive to end him?* "Did you know Mr. McNamara?"

Mr. Montgomery may have been in his nineties, but he was sharp as a tack, his eyes bore into me shrewdly.

"Miss, you'd best change your way of thinkin' if you're thinkin' I killed him."

Slick Fen. Way to go. But the other voice in my head wouldn't leave it alone. In my mind's eye, I saw my grandmother, wagging a finger at me. '*Stand your ground if you want answers. You poked the bear, no time to run away.*'

I looked Earnest *Mick* Montgomery right in the eye, smiled and shook my head, "I never meant to imply anything of the kind, sir. I was just surprised at what you said."

Lester watched Mick and I stare unblinking at each other. He was uncharacteristically quiet.

Mr. Montgomery took a deep breath and blew it out

slowly. "Yeah, I knew Darren McNamara, he was 'bout as worthless as a lump of moldy toe jam. His daddy was the same way, he treated his wife with a heavy hand then he died, and she run off. Darren and his little brother went to live with their auntie, and she raised them out.

"Had a hard time of it though, Darren was always in trouble. He come sniffing around my oldest granddaughter back in the day. My Annie caught wind of it and told me to run him off." He paused to get more coffee. I accepted the refill this time and Lester grinned at me.

Mick continued with his story without any prodding. "So, I was waiting in the bushes when McNamara came to call on my granddaughter. I snatched him up by the collar and told him if he come around again, I would stick my shotgun..."

Lester cleared his throat. Mick seemed to realize what he was about to say was not considered appropriate for a lady's ears. I watched him with wide eyes, willing him to finish the story.

"Um, well I told him to stay the hell away from my granddaughter.

"Shortly after my granddaughter met and married a good guy from up by Springfield, she moved up there and had four children. McNamara never came around anymore but he always hated me after that."

I watched him, took in the sincerity of his story and noticed there wasn't an ounce of emotion in it.

"My granddaughter's four children are all growed up and gave me and my Annie ten great, great grandchildren. They is all spread out between here and Kansas now, but they all come down for the funeral.

It's a good mess of kids." His eyes shown with love and pride for the family that were his descendants. "So, you see Miss, my people came out okay, I didn't have no reason to kill that no-account coward."

"Yes sir, I see what you're saying. But that brings me back to how do you know McNamara is the one that cut your tires?" I probed.

"I reckon he is the only person in this county or the next that hates me. It ain't like I seen him do it, it's the only thing that makes any sense." Mr. Montgomery scooted his chair back from the table and stood up. "It's way past chore time, unless y'all want to help, you best git down the road." He smiled, a mischievous sparkle was back in his eyes.

It was clear to me the interview was over and we were being dismissed. I thanked our host for the coffee and the conversation.

Mr. Montgomery thanked us for the visit. "I don't get many visitors since my Annie died, she was always helping people. Lester, you bring that kid of hers out this spring and we'll tinker with tractors. I've got another old John Deere out back I want to convert to steam."

He stood on the porch and watched us leave.

CHAPTER 11

Lester and I drove along in silence for a few miles. When we reached the blacktop road, my phone notifications went crazy. I debated about pulling over to check them versus heading on home.

Lester asked, "Was that your phone going off? Aren't you gonna check it? Could be important."

There was another dirt road coming up on the right, the mouth of it was quite wide and the perfect place to stop for a moment. I scrolled through the messages, there were six in total. Skipping to the ones from my kids, I read:

Ian: "Hey, you see Mr. M?"

Arista: "LOL" with a picture of the yellow and white kitten standing on Zoey's head while she slept.

I showed the picture to Lester and we both laughed.

Auntie Lou: "You will find more than yourself out in nature today."

I rolled my eyes, *I love my Auntie, ever the Queen of Cryptic Texts.*

There were three from Jacob, 1) "I made the kids

cook and clean up, they let the dice decide. There's chaos in the kitchen so don't be alarmed. 2) Jana's coming over. 3) Where are you? Everything okay?"

I laughed. *My baby brother frets about me.* I thumbed a quick reply to him.

Me: "All good, on way now."

"Lester, do you know it's already 11 a.m.? The time we spent talking with Mr. Montgomery seemed to evaporate." I pulled the truck back onto the road for home.

"Yeah, it is so quiet out there at his place, it didn't seem like almost three hours," Lester agreed.

I parked the truck, and we went in the kitchen door. Jacob wasn't kidding. The kitchen was full of laughter and bantering teenagers. It looked like every pan in the kitchen was dirty.

"Hey, Mom, food is almost ready," Ian said proudly.

Meanwhile, Tom and JJ were pretend sword fighting with tongs. "Ouch, don't pinch me, that's against the rules!" JJ complained.

"Arrgh, there are no rules, ye scoundrel, give up or walk the plank!" Tom said in what I supposed to be a pirate voice.

"Dude, there is no plank! Oh hey, Miss Fen, Mr. Lester." JJ greeted us and got pinched again while he was distracted.

"Okay, you two, you're not eight, if you're going to rough house, take it outside. Don't lose my tongs!" I passed through the kitchen into the family room. Mom sat in the wingback chair beside the fireplace knitting. Jana sat cross legged on the floor in front of the fireplace and Jacob was on the couch reading a tech magazine.

Jacob glanced up from his reading. "Hey sis, you're back! How'd it go?"

I plopped down on the end of the couch. "Not bad, Mr. Montgomery is fine, but he had a lot to say about Darren McNamara." This was enough to pull Jana out of what appeared to be a meditative trance.

"Like what? Do I need to question him? How does he look for the murder?"

Lester ambled in and stood behind the couch, he and I answered in stereo. "He didn't do it."

Jana sighed and made her way to the coffee table. "What makes y'all say that?"

Lester and I took turns filling them in on everything Mr. M. told us, his demeanor, and added commentary about how the conversation felt. When we were done, I asked, "Is there anything new in the investigation?"

Jana stretched and rose from the floor, she took a seat next to Jacob. "I really shouldn't talk about an ongoing investigation, but you're going to hear about it anyway." She cast a meaningful glance at Jacob. He shrugged. "The coroner concluded the cause of death was not being spiked. He found a massive head wound from blunt force trauma. He thinks it happened before McNamara was impaled. He is also running a tox screen but that will take a few days to come back. There was blood that wasn't his on his knuckles."

"Wow, so it sounds like there was a fight and he lost. Has anyone showed up at the hospital with suspicious wounds?" I asked.

"Not yet. There was another strange thing though. The coroner found bite marks that appeared to be several days old. He didn't think they were related, he mentioned them in passing in his report. I took it as indication that our victim was not well liked by man nor beast," Jana said.

"What about the person that burned up in the motor home the other day?" Lester asked.

"That is a whole other mystery. We haven't been able to get an identification on him yet. All the coroner could tell was that it was a male, approximately 20 to 30 years old. The State Police have taken over that investigation because they have more resources but are keeping us in the loop. Nothing has turned up yet. The State Fire Marshall got involved in the investigation and the samples he collected came back positive for chemicals commonly associated with the manufacture of methamphetamine." Jana shook her head.

Jacob shrugged. "If you play with that crap, you're gonna pay a big price, that poor shmuck paid the ultimate price."

"So, is the working theory that the fire victim was the meth cook and it all went wrong?" I asked trying to clarify in my mind what caused the explosion we heard that day.

"That is what the sheriff thinks, and I agree." Jana nodded to emphasize her belief.

Ian hollered from the kitchen. "Food's done!"

The procession of people headed for the kitchen wasn't quite a stampede, though not far from it. I was famished but I hung back to help Mom up out of her chair.

She put her knitting away in the basket and allowed me to help her up. "Ya know, honey, that McNamara kid never was any good. He tried to date your sister, Merriam, when she was sixteen. I thought your daddy was going to kill him then."

I gaped at my mother. "No kidding, Momma? I don't remember hearing any of that!"

"Of course not, dear, you were only six years old. John Peters was a deputy then. He might remember it though. Your daddy gave McNamara a good beating and the old sheriff, I forget his name, arrested both of them, but he let your daddy go. The then sheriff told McNamara to steer clear of the Stonehorse family and leave underage girls alone or he would help hide his body. It was a different time then. Leroy Gibbs, that was the sheriff's name!"

Oh dear, just like that the clear-thinking momma I've always known fades into fantasy. Was the story about daddy true? Alzheimer's sucks so bad.

"Come on, Momma, let's go eat. Ian and the boys cooked, and doesn't it smell wonderful?"

After lunch, I settled Momma back by the fire to resume her knitting. The girls cleaned up the kitchen and complained the boys dirtied every dish in the house. Jana & Jacob planned to head up to Springfield to do some Christmas shopping.

While Jana changed to leave, I took Jacob aside and repeated the story our mother had told me before lunch.

Jacob listened with interest and nodded his head when I got to the part about Daddy beating McNamara up.

"I overheard part of this story once before, but I didn't know the name of the guy involved. Dad and John Peters were sitting around the machine shed, having a beer and were remembering it. They didn't know I was listening. Speaking of our oldest sister, have you talked to her lately?"

"Not since after Thanksgiving. I expect she will call again closer to Christmas," I said.

"Who's going to call at Christmas?" Jana asked, she was walking towards the fireplace patting her coat pockets. "Has anyone seen my keys?"

Jacob's face lit up when he looked at Jana. "Our older sister, Merriam. She's ten years older than Fen, and lives in France, come to think of it you probably never met her. The last time I saw your keys they were on the coffee table." He joined the search for the missing keys.

"France huh? Fancy. What does she do over there?" Jana stopped searching and watched Jacob.

She's a curator of a small museum and she designs dresses on the side, but they are the kind of dresses that models wear while walking down the catwalk. So yeah, you could say our sister is kinda fancy."

I pulled up a picture on my phone and showed it to Jana. "This is the more important and much less fancy side of our big sis."

The photo showed her in a sweatshirt and jeans, no makeup and hair pulled up. She had a fabric measuring tape in one hand, a clipboard in the other and a pencil in her mouth. It wasn't a flattering picture, but it was one of my favorites. "Merriam volunteers teaching orphans and homeless women to sew. She matches the best seamstresses from her classes up with employers she has vetted. She ensures her students get practice by altering and repairing donated clothing in the Dress for Success Worldwide program."

"Wow, that's cool, but why France?"

Jana asked as she sat on the arm of the couch. It appeared she had given up the search for her keys.

"Oh well." I shrugged. "She met a guy, moved to France, the guy split but sis was too broke to leave and too proud to call Momma and Daddy for help, so she stayed and worked. By the time she had enough money to return here, France had become her home."

There was a sudden rattling coming from under the couch. We stared at the floor near the back of the couch. The keys came scooting out from under the heavy couch, propelled by a tiny, clawed paw. The rest of the yellow and white kitten oozed from under the couch and swatted the keys again. They slid across the floor in my general direction.

"My keys!" Jana did a little dance and snatched her keys and the kitten up off the floor. "Good kitty."

She kissed kitty on top of his head, handed the wiggling kitten to me and turned to Jacob.

"Are you ready to roll?"

Jacob bowed. "I am, mademoiselle." He began ushering her in the direction of the kitchen door.

"Oh God, you're going to do the French thing all the way to Springfield, aren't ya."

Effecting his worst French accent, Jacob replied, "Oui, I love all French things. French fries, French toast, French bread, French kissing!"

Jana giggled. "Stop, just stop."

I heard the kitchen door close and looked at the kitten. "You stole those keys to begin with and then took credit for returning them. You, sir, are a grifter."

"Mew?" *And unbelievably cute.*

"Fen, dear, will you bring my knitting basket to my room. I'm gonna move in there, NCIS comes on in five minutes."

Mom tucked her knitting away and hoisted herself out of the chair.

I set the kitten down on the couch. "Sure, Mom."

When I returned to the family room after getting Mom settled in her room with her knitting and a cup of tea, the wayward kitten was nowhere to be seen. I saw my phone laying next to my handbag and I picked it up.

My intention was to read my Kindle app for a while in front of the fire, and when I unlocked the screen the text message from Auntie Lou was front and center. *That's weird, I thought I'd closed the message app. I know the last message I read was from Jacob.* "Huh." I closed the message app and began to read my book, picking up where I left off yesterday at the park.

After I noticed I'd read the same few sentences three times and yet had no idea what they meant I closed the book app and stared at the fire.

The park. I had seen the murder victim at the park the morning of the parade. He was talking to some guys. No, they were arguing. This was no good, I couldn't remember what I heard. I checked the time. *A few more hours of daylight left.* I hopped up, grabbed my handbag and said, "Sophie, come here girl, we're going on an adventure!" My fluffy, black and white dog came flying down the hallway, skidded to a stop at my feet and peered up at me expectantly. "Come on pup, it's been a while since we went walking in town."

I retrieved her bright red harness and matching leash from the peg in the laundry room. The set was leather.

Made and hand tooled by an old friend of my dad's. I added the bling in the form of hand stamped sun and moon conchos and Swarovski crystal beads. It was garish and the dog loved to wear it.

She pranced and bounced to the truck but needed a boost to get in the cab. Sophie peered out the window with excitement and when I pulled into park outside the coffee shop, Cones and Scones she said, "aroo roo roo." I interpreted that as "Oh boy, I'm getting a pup cone!" I'd called our order in to Agatha, so we didn't have to wait long, I had to run in and get my to-go mocha and the small waffle cone of yogurt.

Sophie inhaled her treat. Once she was done, I pulled a wet wipe out of the container in the console and wiped the sticky remnants off my hand. "That was fun huh, let's go check out the park, are you ready?" She wagged and wiggled.

The City Park parking lot was empty when we pulled in. I parked in essentially the same spot as yesterday, hoping to trigger memories of what I had witnessed. *Gosh was that only yesterday? Seems longer ago.* I got out of the truck and lifted Sophie out, it was too far for her to safely jump, though she would have done it. She thinks she is ten foot tall and bullet proof.

I stood looking over the surrounding area. I remembered the red and white truck I now knew belonged to the victim, Darren McNamara. There had been a small dark-colored car, too. I've never been any good at identifying cars just by looking at them, they all look the same unless I can recognize the manufacturers emblem, or the cute name generally emblazoned on the rear.

I walked closer to where the men had been standing.

Sophie watched me and bounced, impatient for the walk she'd been promised. "Wait a minute, pup." I closed my eyes and tried to replay the scene in my head. *What were they saying?*

Sophie began to bark and growl. She pulled as hard as she could on her leash. All the fur on her back bristled up. She'd never done that before. "Sophie, what is your issue?" She stared straight at the dumpster on the right and her little legs were scrambled like a cartoon character, trying to get enough traction to pull me forward.

There was no way I could concentrate on retrieving my memory of the day before when she was losing her mind. "It's probably just a raccoon or an opossum, hopefully not a skunk," I told her, and I trudged forward a few steps and gingerly peeked over the edge of the dumpster.

Once my brain registered what my eyes saw, my body engaged. I screamed and backed up at a run, dragging Sophia back with me. I fell and landed on my rump in the gravel. Desperate to get further away, I scrambled backwards on the ground, the gravel digging into my hands.

Suddenly, strong hands grasped my shoulders, and I screamed again. I came up swinging. I connected with the very surprised face of Dr. Will Spencer. Back on my feet and squared up in a fighting stance I stared at him.

"Whoa, whoa, take it easy, I mean no harm. Are you okay? I heard you scream, are you hurt?" Will held both hands out in front of him. "Fen, what happened?" he asked louder.

Sophia was near my feet, she was squared off,

staring down a very large German Shepherd, who stood next to Will, eyeing me with suspicion and Sophia with mild amusement.

I took a deep breath and dropped my stance. "Call the police, that's not a racoon." And then I fainted.

CHAPTER 12

I was only out for a moment, when I opened my eyes. Will shoved a bottle of water at me and I took a drink. "What happened?"

"You slugged me, said something strange and fainted. Against my better judgment, I did not let you hit the ground." Will rubbed his face. "Dang girl, you pack quite a punch."

"Yeah, sorry 'bout that. Are the police on their way? Is that your dog?" I pointed at the German Shepherd patiently allowing Sophia to sniff him.

"Yep, that's Brutus, and nope I haven't called the police. You were out, and I didn't know what to tell them. All you said was 'that is not a racoon.' Gonna need a little more information."

The town of Blossom Bluff had not switched over to a 911 system yet, so the police department had two main numbers, one for emergencies and one for non-emergencies. Unfortunately, neither phone number was programmed into my phone since I live in the county and therefore in the jurisdiction of the county sheriff's department. I called Sheriff John Peters' cell phone directly. He picked up on the second ring.

"Fenreya, what's wrong? Are the kids okay?" Sheriff Peters was best friends with my dad and was often at our house throughout my childhood. My brother, sister and I all called him Uncle John and, now, so do my kids.

"Uncle John, the kids are fine. I'm at the City Park and I found another body. Please come."

"I will be right there, Fen. Are you safe? Do you have someone with you?"

"Yes, I'm safe and Dr. Will Spencer is here, too."

"Okay, sit tight, I'm on my way."

Sheriff Peters' siren came through the phone before he clicked off the call. I turned and found Will staring at me.

"Did I hear you say, *you found a body*. Like of a human? Where?" Will sounded frantic now. "And the sheriff is your uncle?"

"The sheriff isn't related technically, but yes, he is known as Uncle in my family. Yes, a human, that's what I said before I fainted."

"No, you said, 'it's not a racoon'. There are a bazillion other species to choose from, how was I to translate 'it's not a raccoon' into there is a dead human?" Will rubbed his face again.

"I don't know. Sorry I fainted from shock before making a full report." I knew it was snarky the moment I said it. *Dang it, Fen, you already popped the guy in the face, don't be mean. It's not his fault there is a dead guy in the dumpster...* "Why are you here anyway?" I tried to sound curious rather than accusatory. I watched Will for a reaction or any sign of guile.

"I was running with Brutus. Sunday is the only day the clinic is closed, so we have more time to get some proper exercise in." At the sound of his name, Brutus grinned and thumped his tail.

I finally noticed Will was wearing ¾ length sweats, running shoes and a t-shirt. The t-shirt looked damp with sweat and clung to the muscles in his chest. The high temperature had been a mild 60 degrees today, but it had already started to cool down as the sun slipped steadily closer to the horizon. "Aren't you cold?"

"I wasn't when I was running, but standing around sweaty is getting kinda chilly," he admitted.

I walked to my truck. "I've got a blanket in here," I said over my shoulder.

I rummaged behind the rear seat in my truck and came back with a green and white Indian-style woven blanket. I gave the blanket a good shake and handed it to Will.

He wrapped it across his shoulders. "Thanks, that's better."

We stood in awkward silence for several minutes then began to speak at the same time.

"So."

"What?"

We both laughed.

"You go first," he said.

"What's the deal with Brutus? He's so patient with Sophie." I pointed to the huge dog who was in a relaxed crouch letting little Sophia maul him.

"He flunked out of police dog training, and I took him in. One of my friends in Tucson is a dog trainer at the academy and he made the connection." Will gazed at his dog.

"Flunked out? How can that be? He is clearly an intelligent animal," I said.

"Oh yeah, he is genius level smart, the trouble was he refused to bite anyone. Brutus is a passivist." Will laughed. "It's sad but the dogs in that line of work need to have a bit of controlled aggression to keep themselves and their handlers safe. He doesn't have it. He's great for me, and I would be lost without him."

Brutus rose and took Sophia's leash in his mouth, then he led her over to me and sat down, tail thumping.

I took the leash and picked up Sophia. "You can calm down now, little one, be nice to your new friend."

Will held his hand out for Sophia to sniff, and once he felt accepted, gave her head and ears a friendly ruffle. "She a cutie, what breed is she supposed to be?"

"I got her from a rescue when she was seven weeks old. The mother had been killed, and they had six orphans. The rescue said they thought she was a mix of Shih Tzu, Maltese and something French that I didn't recognize. She's a mutt and a bit of an airhead but she's mine." Sophia grinned and panted.

Sheriff John Peters pulled into the parking lot in his Police issue Ford Interceptor, kicking up a cloud of dust before he came to a stop beside my truck. An ambulance, the coroner and a city police patrol car pulled in behind him.

I sighed. "Here we go."

I hurried to meet the sheriff as he exited his truck, and quickly told him where the body was and how I had come to find it. He took one look in the dumpster and called for the state crime lab to send a team. "Fen, this is going to take most of the night, go on home and we can do a formal statement tomorrow. Is that the new vet over there?"

"Thank you, Sheriff, I love the idea of going home. Yep, that is Dr. Will Spencer, the visiting vet. Come on, I'll introduce you, then I'm outa here." I scooped up Sophia and walked over to where Will stood. "Dr. Will Spencer meet Sheriff John Peters. I'll see you tomorrow, Sheriff."

"Hey, Fen, here is your blanket back."

Will whipped it off his shoulders to hand to me.

I waved him off. "Hang on to it for now, I can get it later." I plopped Sophia in the cab of my truck, hopped in and drove home.

It was dark by the time I pulled into the driveway and parked. Home was such a beautiful sight. The lights were on in the kitchen, and I could see multiple teenagers moving around. I sat there, admiring the concept of home and being grateful for mine. A subtle movement in the laundry room window caught my attention. The silhouette in the window was that of a tiny kitten head. "Check it out, Sophie, how'd he get up in that window?"

She said, "Aroo," and wiggled.

I set her on the ground. As we walked to the door, I watched the kitty in the window. He sat up on his haunches like a groundhog and put his front paws on the glass, while his little eyes followed our progress. I blinked and the kitty disappeared from the window.

The kids practically pounced on me when I walked into the kitchen, they were all talking at once. "Mom, where have you been?"

"We were worried."

"Mom, I've been texting you!"

"Did something happen?"

"Okay kids, let your mom get a word in. Here Fen, figure you could use this." Lester set a steaming cup of fresh coffee on the kitchen island.

"Thank you, Lester, I hope you made a pot, this is a two-cup story."

I grabbed my coffee and headed for the family room and was grateful to see someone, probably Ian, had added logs and kept it going even though it wasn't all that cold outside.

There was something comforting about sitting by a fire. I sat on the couch, kicked off my shoes and tucked my feet under me. My twins, their friends and Lester clustered around, looking eager to hear my tale.

I was distracted momentarily by their faces, there were so many of them. *What am I going to feed them all for supper?* I started to get back up. "This will have to wait till I've figured out some supper."

"Don't worry, Mom, the girls got you. Zoey and Arista heated up the chili and cooked some noodles. We already ate, but we saved you some." Ian patted his stomach as if to emphasize it was full.

"Sorry if you had something else planned, but everyone was hungry and we didn't know where you were," Arista said.

Guilt trip much? I swallowed the hot, soothing brew and thought about my next words. "I left a note, how is it that y'all didn't know where I was?" Kitty sauntered in and climbed up onto my lap and began doing the little toe kneading dance.

"By note, do you mean this?" Ian pulled a torn,

crumpled piece of paper from his hoodie.

I took it from him and noted the only legible words were, "I, Sophie, 4, Chili". Kitty swiped at the note in my hand and I looked down at him. "Did you do this?"

"Mew"

"That was naughty."

"Mew."

I crinkled the paper. The kitten's eyes lit with desire, but he didn't move from my lap, he kept doing his toes on my leg. *Ornery little charmer*.

When I wrote the note it said, "I took Sophie to the park for a walk, be back by four p.m. Chili for supper."

"We deciphered the note enough to think you would be home by four p.m., then you didn't show and then JJ's mom came to pick him up. She said she passed a bunch of emergency vehicles heading toward downtown. When we couldn't get any response on your phone is when we got well and truly worried," Ian explained.

"I'm not sure where my phone is. I had it when I called the sheriff." I dug through my handbag. It was on the coffee table where I haphazardly tossed it. "Ian, would you mind checking the truck for it?"

"Okay, but don't start the story until I get back. Come with me, Tom."

Ian and Tom returned a few short minutes later with my phone. "It was in the backseat."

"Oh, I must have dropped it when I was getting the blanket for Will, that makes sense." I unlocked the screen and browsed notifications. There were several missed texts and four missed calls, all from my kids. "Sorry, kids, I never meant to worry you."

"Who is Will?" Ian and Arista asked in tandem.

"Dr. Will Spencer is the new veterinarian in town. He's filling in while Dr. Johnson is away doing his missionary work. He treated the kittens the other day when I took them in."

"Okay, but why was he at the park with you and what happened?" Arista sounded impatient.

I recounted the entire sequence of events from the time I arrived at the park with only a few interruptions. The kids and Lester peppered the recounting with occasional exclamations of surprise and a few, "Gosh, I'm glad Dr. Spencer was there."

I got up from the couch and headed into the kitchen for more coffee and some food. Lester and four teenagers trailed behind me.

"Mom, who was the dead guy in the dumpster?" Arista asked.

"I can't be 100% sure, but I think it was one of the guys that were arguing with Darren McNamara Saturday morning at the park." I put a handful of tortilla chips in a bowl and ladled some chili over them. "Ian, grab the cheese and sour cream out of the fridge for me, please."

"So, not a local guy," Lester concluded.

I thought about it as I sprinkled grated cheese on top of the chili and added a dollop of sour cream. "I doubt he was local. He was dressed in slacks, a sport coat and city shoes. No one dresses like that here unless they're going to a wedding or a funeral." I took a bite and savored the spicy goodness of the chili. It is always better the next day.

"Gosh, do you think Darren McNamara killed that guy and then stuffed him in dumpster right after you saw them arguing?" Tom asked.

"You were really close to them." Zoey squeaked at the thought.

I realized talking in detail about murder with other people's kids wasn't a stellar idea. "Okay, enough talk of murder. We're all going to leave this alone and let law enforcement take care of it."

I waved a hand to encompass all four kids, "Y'all need to go to bed early. If memory serves, midterm exams are scheduled for the next couple days." I was using my *Mom* voice, the one that means arguments are futile.

There was a chorus of moans and groans of general discontent, but they filed out of the kitchen to their respective rooms until the only people left in the kitchen were Lester and me. He was smirking at me. "What?"

Lester laughed. "We're all going to leave this alone, huh?"

He put the *we* in air quotes. *Since when does he use air quotes, the kids are rubbing off on him.*

"Is that why you made a special trip into town to take a look at the scene so you could remember exactly what you witnessed? That is not a thing someone does who is staying out of something."

Dang it. "Yes, well, um, I see your point, but that was before the second body turned up. I wanted to make sure I was remembering the altercation between McNamara and the two strangers correctly so I could tell Jana and Sheriff Peters." I knew I was reaching and it showed.

Lester shook his head. "Bull feathers. You'll be in this mess up to your neck before you're through. Just be careful and remember to ask for help from time to time.

You can't keep everyone else warm by settin' yourself on fire. I'm going to bed, see ya in the mornin'."

"Good night, Lester, and thanks."

I sat at the kitchen island, lost in thought, sipping coffee which had gotten too cold to be fun to drink when something went skittering across the floor followed by a yellow and white blur. Kitty was having a rousing game of hockey with an unknown object. After a few moments of watching the mighty hunter attacking his prey, I realized the *prey* was a piece of tortilla chip that had gotten away from someone. *Oh dear, I really need to spend some time cleaning this house before it gets away from me entirely.*

I poured out the cold coffee and rinsed my cup. When I walked over to the kitty, he puffed up and hopped sideways, hissing all the way. I picked up the wee cat and the chip, tossed the chip in the trash and cuddled the rowdy little beast. "We need to get you some proper cat toys."

"Mew?"

"Come on, kitty, let's go to bed. You need a name too, what do you think?"

"Merp."

CHAPTER 13

The alarm on my phone blared at six a.m. and it seemed as though no time had passed since my head hit the pillow. Isabella was asleep on my feet and little Mr. Hissy Face was curled up on my chest. *Geez, no wonder I didn't move all night.*

It took me several minutes to convince myself to dislodge the felines and leave my cozy bed to start my day. Sophia and Violet met me in the kitchen at the door, they wanted out. I noticed Jacob's car in the driveway. *Huh, wonder what time he got home and if Jana is with him?* With the dogs out and coffee underway, I surveyed the contents of the fridge and the state of my kitchen. Both were a mess. I sighed. *Coffee first.*

I was on my second cup when Lester ambled out of his room, he let the dogs in and poured a cup for himself. Noting that he looked a little rough this morning I said, "Good morning, did you sleep well?"

He managed a dim smile. "No, I didn't, my cast itched me through the night, and I couldn't stop frettin'."

"Sorry to hear it. Hey, don't you have a doctor appointment today? Maybe they'll take the cast off."

"It's tomorrow at 10 a.m. At least once the cast is off, I can start driving again and I won't be such a burden around here."

"Stop right there, mister. You are not now, nor have you ever been a burden. I've liked having you stay with us, and I know the kids feel the same way. Frankly, I'll be sad when you go home, but I'm sure you'll be relieved to be back in your own home," I said.

"Aw go on with ya, I'll only be down the road. I might come up here every day or so to pester ya', you know, for old times' sake," Lester said gruffly.

Jacob wandered into the kitchen, bleary eyed in t-shirt and sweatpants. "Thank the gods, there's coffee."

"Hey, bro, you look like something the cat dragged in, what time did you get home?" I asked.

Jacob glared at me and poured the last of the coffee into a cup.

"Around one a.m. Shopping in Springfield is not for the faint of heart, the traffic was terrible, and the mall was jam packed with people."

I glanced at Lester and winked. "Ya know, if you take the last of the coffee, you gotta make another pot, that's a rule."

Jacob growled a little but set about making a new pot. "I heard you had some excitement yesterday. You've become a magnet for trouble, sissy."

"Yeah, but you love me anyway. Is Jana here? If I'm going to tell the story again, she may as well hear it too," I said.

"No, I dropped her off last night at her place. She

had to go in early due to the new developments. I'm going to meet her for lunch, you should come along," Jacob said.

"That could work, I have no idea what I'm doing today but a trip to the grocery store is imminent." I sighed.

The kitchen filled up as four teenagers thundered in, talking and laden with backpacks, jackets and assorted musical instruments. Tom played the saxophone and was quite good and Zoey played the violin very well. My twins, although musically talented, opted not to play instruments for school although their friends had been working on them, trying to get them to join either the band or the orchestra. I have always believed in letting my kids choose their extracurricular activities, the only caveat is, whatever they pick they have to stick with it for the school year. No quitting just because it's hard.

After a few moments of chatting and saying goodbyes, they rushed out to meet the school bus. School breakfast on Mondays was always cinnamon rolls, sausage links and eggs. The eggs were nothing special, but the cinnamon rolls were the real deal, made by an ancient and very sweet little lady who had worked in the cafeteria since God was young.

Once the kids left, Jacob disappeared back to the room he used when he was here, and I headed for the gym downstairs. I needed to find a direction for the day and settling my mind first was the only way.

After an hour of stretching, sweating and a mile on the elliptical machine and the hottest shower I could stand, I had a plan for the day. Little did I know how futile the plan was.

We were in for another unseasonable warm day in the sixties. I couldn't help but think we would pay for this lovely weather next month. I dressed in jeans, a tie dye t-shirt of Arista's creation and a denim jacket, grabbed my phone and handbag and out the door I went. I met Lester coming back from the barn. "I'm off to do the grocery shopping, if you think of anything you need let me know."

Lester dusted the uncasted hand on his bib overalls. "Will do, stock is fed, getting low on range cubes. I think I'll go have a look at the side by side. Ian mentioned it was running a bit rough."

"Okay, thanks Lester, see ya later."

About halfway to town my phone rang, the screen on the dash of the truck showed Sheriff John Peters' number so I accepted the call. "Hey, Sheriff, what's up?"

"Good morning, Fen, can you come by the station? I need a formal statement about yesterday and I was wondering if you remembered anything else about Saturday."

"I'm already on my way to town, so I can swing by and yes, I did. I'd planned to call you later about that very thing. See you shortly."

I popped into Cones and Scones and grabbed a box of mixed mini pastries and a Carmel Macchiato then proceeded over to the sheriff's office.

Rachel was at the front desk on the phone, and she waved me back towards the sheriff's office. I tapped on the frame of the open door and Uncle John motioned for me to come inside. He was also on the phone.

I placed the box of pastries on his desk and flipped the lid open, revealing the assortment of sticky goodness.

I plopped down in the chair in front of his desk, I selected a cheese Danish and tried to appear as if I wasn't eavesdropping.

"I understand your concern, Ms. Paulson.

"Yes, I agree. It's rude for your neighbors to allow their dogs to do their business in your yard, unfortunately it isn't against the law.

"Yes, I know Chief Jenkins used to do things differently. No one misses him more than I do.

"Yes ma'am, it's a shame.

"Uh huh, uh huh, perhaps you could attend the next city council meeting and bring that up?

"Uh huh, okay.

"I have someone in my office now, gotta go." Click.

Sheriff Peters heaved out a breath and leaned back in his chair. "Good gravy, I don't know how the chief put up with all these town type problems. The woman on the phone calls every other day with some new drama. She isn't the only one!" He selected a cherry Danish and took a bite.

"Why are you handling the police department matters? Don't they have jurisdiction on everything that happens within the city limits?" I asked, wiping my fingers on my jeans and wishing I had thought to grab some napkins.

Uncle John passed a partial roll of paper towels across the desk to me.

"Yes, city matters fall under the auspices of the city police department, however, you may have heard that Chief Daniels retired suddenly for medical reasons last week. The mayor and county commissioner got together and decided that I would take over running the police department temporarily, in addition to my regular sheriff duties until a *suitable replacement* for the chief can be found."

"Jeepers, I hope they doubled your salary if you're doing the work of two people."

He rolled his eyes. "Yeah, right." Uncle John grabbed an apple Danish. "Don't tell Celeste about the pastries, I'm supposed to be watching my sugar."

I gave him a thumbs up. "I spent some time thinking about what all I saw Saturday morning. I think the guy in the dumpster was one of the guys I saw arguing with Darren McNamara on Saturday."

Sheriff Peters sat up in his chair, set aside his pastry and grabbed pen and paper. "Tell me everything."

Starting at when I pulled into the parking lot and unloaded BB on Saturday morning, I recounted every detail to Sheriff Peters.

"And you heard the guy say what again?" he asked.

"The shorter of the two men said, 'Where's our stuff, Cabrón?' Then McNamara said, 'I don't know, I don't have it. It prolly burned up with that idiot.' Next dumpster guy grabbed him by the shirt and gave him a shake. 'Our boss will not like that answer, you are going to have to do better.'

"Then there was a scuffle and one of the guys, the bigger one I think, mumbled something to his partner but the only words I could make out were, El Jefe."

Sheriff Peters tossed his pen down and leaned back in his chair. "Huh, sounds to me like our Mr. McNamara was tangled up with some Mexican drug dealers. The *stuff* they referred to was something of value to them, wouldn't have to be drugs, but the comment about 'burning up' makes me think of the RV fire. There was trace evidence consistent with meth at the fire scene."

I watched as Sheriff Peters picked up his pen and drew a diagram of sorts on a piece of paper.

"You think they are Mexican drug dealers because of the smattering of Spanish words I overheard?" I asked.

"Yes. Fen, you need to hear and understand what I'm about to say to you. If my theory is correct, there are some very bad people at play here. You need to stay out of this, keep your brother and kids out of it, too. Do you understand?"

I felt sixteen again and got caught toilet-papering the principal's house with my friends. "Yes, sir, I got it."

"Good girl, now take these Danishes with you before my wife walks in and catches me abusing my sugar quota." The sheriff grinned. His phone rang, he frowned and reached to answer it.

I grabbed the box of pastries, waved goodbye and left his office. On the way past Rachel's desk, I overheard her.

"You found a what? A finger! Oh dear. Please hold for the sheriff."

My mind spun with possibilities when I hopped behind the wheel of my truck. *My stars! A human finger? What else could it be? And where?* The phone in my pocket literally roared to life. The notification bubble revealed two new messages, one from Jacob.

"Lunch is delayed, Jana called away. Call me when you can."

The second came from Auntie Lou, I groaned. *Goddess, I love that woman and my day wouldn't seem complete without a baffling message from her.* I opened the text and read it.

"The world is ripe with opportunities for good and ill, choose wisely."

I sighed and closed the text app, then I called Jacob.

"Hey sis, you still want to have lunch? I'm starving and already in town."

"Sure, how about the Tortilla Shack on Flower Road?" I suggested. The pastries had only ramped up my hunger and if I went grocery shopping in my current state, it would be an ugly bill.

"Sounds good, see you there," Jacob said and clicked off the call.

I drove up the business loop and took a right where it intersected with Flower Road to go east. The Tortilla Shack sat down a ways on the right, near the corner of Pine Street. Jacob was already there, and I pulled into an open spot next to his car. We were about to go inside the restaurant when sirens split the relative quiet. We watched as the sheriff's truck came screaming up Flower Road, slowed for traffic and made a left to go north on Pine Street.

Jacob said, "Dang! Wonder what happened now?" He opened the door for me.

"I have an inkling of an idea, let's grab a table and I'll tell you what I heard. Where is Jana anyway?" I surveyed the inside of the restaurant for the best place to sit and not be overheard.

"Only two today," Jacob said to the hostess when she came bearing menus and rolls of silverware. To me he said, "She's working an accident out on the highway. A tractor trailer hauling a load of furniture capsized and scattered furniture everywhere. No one was hurt, but it is a huge mess."

"Bummer." I sat in the booth in the rear corner of the dining room and opened my menu. The daily special was Enchiladas Verde with beans and rice, plus choice of beef or chicken. We both chose the special with chicken. Once the waiter left to fill our order, I said, "When I was leaving the sheriff's office, I heard Rachel take a call about someone finding a finger, like only a finger! I think that must be where the sheriff went."

"Yikes, that's gross. Ever since you and Merry made me watch Jaws when I was little, I can't handle dismembered anything." Jake shuddered.

"Yeah, bro, if it's any consolation I do feel bad about it in hindsight."

Chips, salsa and the side of Queso Dip Jacob ordered materialized on our table. Our wait person was so efficient we barely noticed their comings and goings. I took a chip and loaded it with creamy cheese dip.

"Too little too late, sissy." Jake stuffed a chip laden with queso in his mouth.

He winked to let me know he wasn't really harboring a grudge.

The food was good, with the right amount of spicy heat. I suspended all talk of murder and body parts for my brother's benefit.

As we finished up, Jacob asked, "Where are you off to next?"

The words *grocery store,* were barely out of my mouth when my phone rang loudly. I hurried to silence it so it wouldn't disturb the other diners. "Oh oh, it's Arista. School is still in session, she never calls." I answered, "Hey, honey, are you okay?"

My daughter's words tumbled over themselves. "Mom, you have to come now, Brandy's been arrested! She didn't do it, Mom, please come."

CHAPTER 14

"I'll be right there." I clicked off the call, rising to leave. Jacob stared at me expectantly, he didn't have to wait long.

"Arista has summoned me to the school, Brandy has been arrested, presumably for killing McNamara, although she didn't say that. She is frantic. Are you coming?"

"You know I am. I'll drive." Jacob paid the bill, tipped the guy and told them we'd be back for my truck in a little while.

Jacob got to the high school in record time. He told me later he figured all the cops were otherwise engaged so getting a speeding ticket wasn't a high concern. He slid into the lot at the school, and I bailed out of the sporty little car. Deputy Clyde Young stood by his car surrounded by my daughter and about twenty other students. A teacher whom I liked but couldn't recall her name right then was also there. I charged in.

"Deputy Young, what is going on? Why are you arresting Brandy and where is her mother?" I went nose to nose, well nose to forehead with the least-liked deputy in the county.

"Fenreya Stern, mind your own business, this is a police matter."

"Mom, he burst into class and yelled she was under arrest for the murder of Darren McNamara! *Mom*, he *handcuffed* her and dragged her out of class!" I couldn't remember seeing Arista so angry, not since Ian superglued her doll to a remote-controlled boat and launched it at the lake when they were seven.

"Deputy, what evidence do you have? Thinking that wisp of a girl could somehow get that big man impaled on a spike is preposterous!" I shook my head.

"Oh, are you a lawyer now, Fenreya, instead of just a nosy busy body?" Clyde retorted although I had seen a glimmer of doubt when I pointed out the obvious lack of physical power for his suspect to get the job done.

"No, Clyde, I'm not a lawyer, I am a concerned parent who cares what happens in this community."

"What is the meaning of all this!" I turned to see the source of the question. The *Dog Lady*. I mean Superintendent Vanderkamp, charged across the parking lot in her high heels. If I hadn't been so mad it would have been amusing. She shrieked questions. "Mrs. Parsons, why are all your students out of class? And YOU, (she was looking at me) WHY are YOU here?"

Before I could form an answer Jacob put a steadying hand on my arm and Mrs. Parsons spoke up. "My students have been studying civil disobedience, peaceful protest and due process and this debacle is what we call a teachable moment, Madame Superintendent." *Ah, now I remember why I like that teacher.*

The superintendent sputtered. "That'll be enough of that, all you get back inside the school." She whirled on me so aggressively I automatically dropped one foot behind me in a subtle fighting stance. Jacob gripped my arm tighter.

"You are not the accused's parent and therefore have no business on school property at this time." She pointed at me and Jacob. "You both need to leave at once."

Deputy Clyde Young smirked, the heat was off him and he was enjoying the show. I ignored him and the wretched Vanderkamp woman. I turned my attention to the squad car. Brandy sat in the backseat, handcuffed. Her big eyes watched me even as tears rolled down her face. Arista and her band of contentious students parted like the red sea to allow me to get closer to Brandy's window. "Brandy, honey, I'm going to get your mom. Don't say anything to anyone until she shows up. Do you hear me?"

She nodded but didn't say anything.

Clyde Young shoved me away from his car. "That's enough Stern."

Jacob stepped between me and the deputy. "Clyde, don't ever put your hands on my sister again."

"Are you threatening an officer of the law, Stonehorse?" Clyde sneered. "There's room in the car for one more."

Jacob didn't budge. "Not at all, deputy, I wouldn't dream of threatening an esteemed member of law enforcement. But I'm not the one you should worry about."

This last bit clearly went over Clyde's head. He scoffed and got in his squad car.

Mrs. Parsons began to herd her class back toward the school, Arista hung back watching me. I mouthed, "It will be okay, go back to class." I turned and found Superintendent Vanderkamp eyeing me.

Without a word she spun and stalked back across the gravel parking lot in her high heels, wobbling and muttering under her breath.

Jacob huffed out a held breath. "Wow, that woman is absurd and she really hates you. What'd you do besides show up here today?"

"I was nice to her obnoxious little dog, and I make a better pot of chili than she does, other than that I have no idea. Can we drive over to the nursing home? I want to see if I can find Brandy's mom, and I don't have her phone number."

"Of course, hop in."

Jacob drove a more temperate pace to the nursing home and elected to wait in the car while I went in. If I found Brandy's mom, we didn't want her to feel ganged up on. I went to the reception desk inside the door and realized I had no idea what Brandy's last name was or if her mom even had the same last name. *Oh dang, I'm unprepared for this mission.*

The receptionist smiled a 100 watt smile. "Hi, how can I help you?"

Rather than seem like a complete moron, I stuck my

phone to my ear and said, "Hello," making an *I'm so sorry face* at the receptionist, I held up a finger and retreated back out the door. Outside I fired off a text to Arista. "Quick, what's Brandy's mom's name?" Seconds later the reply came. "Tammy Turner."

I re-entered the nursing home and the receptionist's smile dimmed to about 40 watts. She raised her eyebrows and said, "May I help you?"

I adopted my most unassuming smile. "Gosh I sure hope so, I need to talk to Tammy Turner, and I've misplaced her phone number. Would she be around?"

"We don't disclose employee's whereabouts, it's company policy." She pursed her lips.

"I totally understand, it's just that our daughters go to school together and we accidently received Mrs. Turner's order of cookie dough from the recent fund raiser, it's perishable and I haven't been able to connect with her." It was lame and I knew it.

"Can't the girl take it home?" The receptionist's tone inferred I was some kind of idiot for not thinking of that. Perhaps I was. *I suck at this.*

I turned up my smile and rolled my eyes. "Oh, you know how teenagers are."

The name badge hanging from the receptionist's neck read Amanda.

"Please, Miss Amanda, can't I speak with Tammy for a tiny second, then I promise to get out of your hair." I smiled and visualized her picking up the phone and summoning Tammy to the front. I'm not sure if it was the deferential, "Miss Amanda," or the promise to go away that won Amanda over, but she picked up her little walkie talkie and said, "Tammy Turner, please report to the front desk for a visitor."

"Thank you, you're awesome." I backed away from the desk to an area of the lobby where I could see the three diverging hallways simultaneously.

A few minutes later, the young woman I had seen sitting with Brandy Saturday morning at the coffee shop came tentatively up the hall. She seemed to relax a little when she saw me.

"Hello, do I know you?" She had a black eye. It was poorly covered with makeup.

"Hi, Ms. Turner, I'm Fen Stern, Arista's mom. Can we talk somewhere private?"

"What's this about? Is Brandy okay?" Tammy's voice had ratcheted up a bit. Amanda eyed us with thinly veiled annoyance.

I don't want to lie to this woman. I need her to trust me. I was trying to avoid making a scene at her workplace, so I said, "She's okay but she needs her mom. I really need to talk with you, and it should be a quiet conversation." I took her hand gently in both of mine. "Please Tammy."

Tammy narrowed her eyes and pulled her hand back, but she cast a glance at Amanda. "Amanda, I'll be back in a moment." Neither of us paid any attention to Amanda's response or lack thereof. We stepped outside.

"What is this about?" Her voice spoke of distrust and defensiveness. *Oh boy, this is going to be harder than I thought.*

"There is no easy way to say this, Brandy was arrested at school for murdering Darren McNamara." I rushed on in spite of the horrified, frenzied look on her face and the questions started to form. "The deputy who arrested her isn't known for his brains, and I doubt the sheriff even knew it was happening. Nevertheless, she needs you and a lawyer at the station. I told her not to talk to anyone until you got there." I paused to let that sink in and watched as the color drained from her face. Tammy sunk heavily into the wrought iron bench beside the door and began to cry.

Tammy was still crying and rocking on the bench when the charge nurse came outside to investigate. I recognized her immediately and more importantly she remembered me from the time my mother was in this facility for rehab after the vehicle accident.

She was a stocky built, older lady. I figured her nerves were steel and her heart was gold. She took in the scene and melted into the bench by Tammy. "Oh, Tammy honey, what's happened? Is it your daughter? Your momma?" She patted and rubbed Tammy's back like one might comfort an infant. Having received no intelligible answer, the nurse, Ruth, cast a questioning look my way.

"There is a family crisis, no one is injured but she really needs to leave work early today and attend to some things. I hope to be able to help her resolve it quickly."

Dang, where did that come from? What am I going to do? So much for staying out of this mess. Meh, it's not like I promised the sheriff I would stay out of it and that was before all this happened.

Nurse Ruth eyed me, searching my face for any sign of guile. I watched her jaw set as her decision was made.

She gave Tammy a gentle shake. "Tammy, you go with Fen, she is good people. Don't worry about your job, I got you. You go do whatever needs doing and call me tomorrow. I'm going to run in and get your purse."

Ruth came back in a flash with Tammy's handbag and a ratty looking denim jacket with faux sheep wool around the collar. "Come on, let's get you up and moving."

Tammy nodded mutely and stood up. Ruth handed her off to me and I led her to Jacob's car. Silently, I wished it was a four door. Jake must have read my mind. He got out and came around the car. "Hi, I'm Fen's brother, we're going to take you to Brandy."

I folded myself into the backseat and Jacob saw Tammy safely seated in front and closed her door. Moments later we were headed for the Sheriff's Department.

Tammy wiped her nose on her sleeve, and I winced. Jacob opened the center console and dug out a handful of paper napkins, the kind you get from fast food joints.

It's always good to have a supply of those on hand.

Tammy mumbled "thanks" and mopped her face. Her mascara had run and the makeup that was supposed to disguise the black eye was gone. The poor lady looked like a raccoon. A sad one. She mumbled, "Oh god, I knew something like this would happen. I should have left him. She was so angry, she hated him."

I leaned up from the backseat, not believing what I heard. "Wait a minute, do you actually think your daughter killed Darren McNamara?"

"I, I don't know what to think. I know she hated him. I know she has been telling me to leave him for months. What if she did?"

"How about innocent until proven guilty? How about you believe in your daughter until you have all the facts?" My voice grew louder. Jacob caught my eye in the rear-view mirror and shook his head ever so slightly. I ignored him.

Tammy wheeled on me, as best she could while seat-belted into the tiny bucket seat. "What do you know about my daughter, or me? Why do you even care?"

"You're right, I don't know your daughter very well, but I know MY daughter and she believes with her whole heart that your daughter is innocent, and I believe in her. That is also why I care."

The car remained silent the rest of the way to the station. Once Jacob pulled in and found a spot near the door, we all got out. Tammy had composed herself over the last few minutes. "I'm sorry I snapped at you, that was rude. It appears you are trying to help us, and I thank you. What do I do now?"

I took hold of both her hands. "Now we walk in there and see exactly why they arrested her. We know the sheriff. He is a good man and will give her a fair shake.

"We avoid talking to Deputy Clyde Young because he is a dolt, and if they are intent on keeping your daughter locked up, we find you an attorney." I turned loose of her hands and took off walking towards the building's entrance.

I heard Tammy say to Jake, "Your sister is kind of intense, has she done this before?"

Jacob laughed. "Not this exactly, but let's say it ain't her first rodeo."

I walked into the sheriff's department for the second time in one day and came face to face with Clyde. "What're you doin' here, Stern?" he sneered.

"I'm coming to see Sheriff Peters, and I've got the mother of the girl you erroneously arrested with me.

You know, the one you should have called because the girl is a MINOR." I turned my attention to Rachel, who was at her desk and watching my interaction with Clyde. "Rachel, if Sheriff Peters is in, may we see him?"

She waved me back even though Clyde said, "Hey, you can't go back there!"

A voice boomed out of the adjacent office, even before the sheriff's frame filled the doorway. "Yes, Deputy Young, they most certainly can. Now you go to your desk and finish filling out the arrest report. I want it on my desk in fifteen minutes."

"But Sheriff—" Clyde whined. He didn't get to finish his argument.

Sheriff Peters pointed. "You, desk, report, now. No buts."

I hid my smile as the sheriff welcomed me, Tammy and Jacob into his office.

Introductions were made and we sat down. Tammy fidgeted with the hem of her smock. "When can I see my daughter, sir?"

"In a few moments. First, I want to explain what has happened and what needs to happen next." Sheriff Peters leaned forward at his desk and let his hands rest on the desk, palms up. His body language told me he was about to put his cards on the table and was open to receive any information available.

"Earlier today, while I was out at another scene, Deputy Young received an anonymous tip. It detailed the whereabouts of the alleged murder weapon used to kill Darren McNamara. Deputy Young dispatched himself to the scene and did retrieve a softball bat bearing an inscription with your daughter's name.

Deputy Young secured the bat in an evidence bag and proceeded directly to the high school where he placed Brandy under arrest. Had I been kept abreast of the situation, it would have been handled much differently. However, that ship has sailed."

I started to list all the things wrong with the situation, but the sheriff held up a hand to stop me. He wasn't done.

"As I was saying, the arrest has been made. No one has questioned Brandy successfully. He looked at me and smiled. "I have spoken with the judge, and she has agreed Brandy should be released into your custody, pending the results of assorted forensic tests. I will tell you that neither you nor your daughter can leave the county because she is at best a material witness and at worst a suspect in the homicide of Darren McNamara. Bail will not be required at this time."

Tammy visibly relaxed. She appeared to be speechless. I had questions. "Sheriff Peters, when you say that Brandy is still a suspect, does that mean she needs an attorney? Anonymous tip sounds awfully suspicious, is someone besides Clyde attempting to substantiate the tip?"

Sheriff Peters sighed. "Given the circumstances, a lawyer would be a good idea. If you know one, you'd like to use, call them, if not, here is the phone number for the Public Defender's office." He pushed a business card across the desk to Tammy. She took it and pocketed it. The sheriff continued, "Yes, Fen, I have my best investigator working on the tip. Ms. Turner, do you have any questions for me right now?"

"No sir, except can I take my daughter home now?"

"Yes, you can, and here is my direct phone number,

use it as needed with questions or information. If my Deputy Jana Smith contacts you, you may rely on what she says."

The sheriff picked up his desk phone. "Deputy Sharp, please bring Miss Brandy Turner up to my office. Do not let her be detained any longer. Uh huh, yep, thanks." He hung up the phone. "She will be right up, Ms. Turner."

"Johnny is working the jail?" I asked with disappointment. Deputy Johnny Sharp impressed me last month during all the drama as being an intelligent, professional young man, and it seemed a waste to have him babysit at the county jail.

"Only temporarily, Dennis is out with the flu. Deputy Sharp will be back on patrol within the next few days," Sheriff Peters explained patiently. He knew my entire family thought highly of the young man.

Deputy Young opened the door and poked his head in the office. "Here is the arrest report you wanted, sheriff."

"Deputy Young, do not barge into my office without knocking. Please give the report to Rachel and go out on traffic patrol. Now."

"Yes, sir." Dejected, Deputy Young turned to go and visibly bristled at the sight of Deputy Sharp escorting Brandy down the corridor from the stairway that led to the jail. He started to turn back towards the sheriff and was cut off.

Sheriff Peters said, "Not a word, Young."

Tammy rose to her feet, and in a hot second, had her daughter wrapped in a hug. They were both crying.

I did not hide my smile. "Thank you, Sheriff. I'm curious about the incident that had you blazing lights and sirens over by Pine Street."

Sheriff Peters held up a hand to stop me. "I'm sure you are curious about that, and I will remind you of our earlier conversation, you remember? The one where I advised you to stay out of this and you agreed. Besides, it's been a long day, it's going to get longer, and I will be lucky if I get to see Celeste before midnight. Please go home, hug your kids, and stay out of trouble."

Jacob stepped in. "Come on sis, I think Tammy and Brandy would like to be anywhere but here and we're their ride."

With that, we all filed out of the station and piled into Jacob's tiny car. "Tammy, I assume your car is over at the nursing home, shall we swing by there first?" Jacob shifted into reverse to exit the parking spot.

"Um, my car is at home, broke down. I caught a ride in with one of the aides, but she won't be leaving work for hours." Tammy sounded downtrodden.

"No worries, I can drive y'all home. Drop us at my truck, Jake."

Thirty minutes later I pulled my truck into Tammy's driveway. She had been quiet during the drive and Brandy was texting up a storm in the backseat, undoubtedly with my daughter. I was surprised to find they lived only a couple miles from us, as the crow flies, on a dirt road that makes a long lazy loop off the road Stonehorse Ranch is on.

The house appeared small and in need of paint, the yard packed full of junk. Tammy noticed me noticing and blushed. "Darren was a slob. Now, if we stay here, we can pick it up." Her voice trailed off.

"There must be a lot of uncertainty and stress for you right now. I hadn't said it before, but I'm sorry for your loss. Had you and Darren been together long?"

"Too long," Brandy exclaimed as she climbed down from the truck and slammed the rear door. She started for the house.

"Wait Brandy!" Tammy pointed at the house. Her hand shook. "I shut the door and locked it when I left for work. Don't go in there."

CHAPTER 15

Brandy stopped about halfway to the house. I got out of the truck. I had retrieved my Maglite from my center console and stalked towards the open door.

Tammy jumped out of the truck. "What are you doing? Fen, are you going in there?"

"Yep, wait here." I wasn't exactly frightened, cautious, would be a good description. I stood and considered the house, the door and surrounding yard. We were out in the boonies, there were no other vehicles present so if someone was there, they would have walked in. That seemed wholly unlikely.

I took up a position to the side of the door, like they do on TV but minus the ubiquitous gun, and flipped on my big flashlight and stuck it around the door jamb. There was no reaction to the light, so I peeked. *Oh dear.* "Tammy, come look at this, I don't suppose you left it this way either. We need to call the sheriff."

The inside of the house was wrecked, cushions off the couch and chairs were cut open and every drawer visible was open or emptied onto the floor.

Tammy took one look and visibly paled, I thought she may faint, so I sat her on the only thing handy, a five-gallon bucket. Brandy trotted over and peered in the house. "WTH who did this?" She placed protective hands on her mom's shoulders.

I clicked off my call to the sheriff and ushered Brandy and her mom back to my truck to wait. I also called Jacob and told him what was going on. He offered to come out but instead I asked him to find something to feed a bunch of people dinner, maybe subs. I had dismissed the notion of grocery shopping a couple hours ago and knew there was nothing fixed at the house in the quantity that would be needed. I suspected we would have two more people at the house tonight.

We sat in my truck waiting in silence. Brandy and her mom appeared stunned, angry and scared. I rolled the implications of this new development around in my head. I had questions but they were essentially the same ones I knew the sheriff would ask, so I held my tongue. It only took about 20 minutes for Sheriff Peters to arrive in his Ford Interceptor. Deputy Jana Smith pulled in behind him in her personal truck. Jana was still in uniform but must be off duty and likely heading to my house to meet up with Jacob. She undoubtedly volunteered to back the sheriff up on her way.

We continued to wait while Sheriff Peters and Jana cleared the house. They walked over to my truck where we sat with the windows down halfway. Tammy told Brandy to wait in the truck as she and I both climbed out of the front seat.

"Ladies, we meet again," said Sheriff Peters, "did any of y'all go in the house when you got here?" He eyed me when he spoke. We hadn't and told him so. "Okay, here's what has to happen, Tammy, I want you and Brandy to do a walk through with Captain Smith. She will be taking photos. List anything that's missing but please try not to touch anything except your clothes and toiletries. Pack some stuff, you're not staying here tonight." He peered at the isolated property, there wasn't even a security yard light. "Pack enough for a few days."

Tammy started to object. "We don't have the money for a room, my mom lives in Springfield, but the car is broke."

I waved a hand. "Tammy, you will both stay with us, we have room. It's no trouble so just say yes."

Brandy smiled for the first time all day. "Cool, Mom, you will love their house."

"I guess for tonight, thank you, Fen, you've done so much all ready," Tammy said.

"Ms. Turner, are y'all ready to do that walk through with me?" Jana had her digital camera hanging around her neck and a clipboard in her hand.

"Yes, ma'am." Tammy and Brandy followed Jana into their ransacked house.

Once they were out of earshot, I turned to the sheriff, "This is not a coincidence. What do you suppose they were looking for?"

Sheriff Peters shrugged. "Could be anything, money, drugs, guns? I don't suppose the Turners mentioned anything of interest while y'all were waiting on me?"

"Not a peep and I didn't question them because I knew you would want to go first," I said proudly.

"First? Fenreya, you admit you'll be questioning them at some point," he smirked. "There is no point in me telling you not too. Those ladies seem a bit skittish, maybe they will tell you things they won't tell me. What do you make of Tammy's black eye?"

"I'm certain Darren McNamara gave her that shiner. Oh, I think I told you about seeing her and Brandy at the coffee shop Saturday morning."

The sheriff's face held the question and he circled his hand in the universal, *please go on,* sign. I filled him in.

Sheriff Peters nodded and rubbed his stubbly chin thoughtfully. "You know that's motive. Abused women have been known to snap and strike back at their abuser."

"Yeah, I know Uncle John, but wasn't Tammy at work when Darren was killed?"

"Pretty sure I read that in Jana's initial report, but I will follow up. Could be motive for Brandy, too, saving her momma from an abusive man." He held up a hand when I bristled. "I know, Fen, I'm thinking out loud. Listen, I know you're not going to leave this alone so do me a favor and keep an eye on them."

Tammy and Brandy walked back over to where I stood with Sheriff Peters. They both had duffle bags slung over their shoulders.

Sheriff Peters eyed them. "I'll need you both down at the station for formal statements tomorrow. Brandy should have a lawyer with her as we discussed. Jana and I will secure your house once she is done taking photos. Please avoid going back in there until we have released it as a crime scene. Do you have everything you need for a few days?"

Tammy winced but answered in the affirmative and Brandy nodded. She put their bags in the back of my truck.

"Ladies, can either of you think of anything the perpetrator might have been looking for in your house?"

Both of them answered, "No, sir."

"Ms. Turner, did Darren McNamara live here? It isn't his address of record."

"He stayed here most of the time, I don't know where he stayed when he wasn't here." Tammy frowned.

"Okay, you can all go. Get some rest, you've all had quite the day. I'll see you tomorrow." *Sheriff Peters, king of the kind dismissal.* He had work to do. It had been quite the day for him too.

"Let's go, ladies, I have it on good authority that there is food waiting at the house and Arista is about to turn herself inside out wanting to see you, Brandy." I hoped my upbeat tone would lift their spirits.

Arista and Ian met us in the driveway. Ian retrieved the duffle bags out of the truck and hauled them in the house. Arista grabbed Brandy by the hand, and they disappeared into the house, likely heading for Arista's room. Tammy appeared lost.

"Come on in, Tammy, I'll give you the nickel tour and get you settled in your room. I suspect Brandy will want to stay with Arista." I smiled encouragingly. Tammy followed me into the kitchen.

Lester put a steaming cup of coffee on the kitchen island. "Hey Fen, figured you could use this. Hi, I'm Lester, you must be Brandy's momma. Do you drink coffee?" *Bless him.*

Tammy nodded. "Yes, sir, I like coffee, it's nice to meet you." She looked overwhelmed but who could blame her after the whirlwind of emotions and events of the day.

"Have a seat, Lester makes a great cup of coffee. I'll be right back."

I headed through the family room and down the hall to my room to drop off my purse and grab a moment of solitude. I heard shrieking coming from Arista's room, the happy kind, not the *omg the sky is falling again* kind. I smiled. *Quality time with Arista is exactly what poor Brandy needs right now. So young.*

I headed back to the kitchen. Lester had engaged Tammy in pleasant conversation as she sipped her coffee. It was the first time she had looked at ease since I invaded her workday a few hours ago. Ian stared in the open fridge. "Honey, shut the door, you're letting all the cold out."

"But Mom, I'm starving." He'd drawn out the words to emphasize the dire nature of his hunger.

"I know, honey, you're practically wasting away. I'm surprised your Uncle Jacob isn't back yet, he's bringing food."

"Thank god." Ian closed the fridge and began rummaging in the cupboard where the crackers, chips and cookies were kept. I rolled my eyes.

Arista and Brandy came running into the kitchen. Brandy had the black and grey kittens clutched to her chest. She grinned from ear to ear. "Momma, look! It's them!" She thrust the kittens at her mother.

Tammy melted, "Oh my gosh! Where have you been? We thought you were dead!"

She cast about the room, searching for an explanation.

"They turned up in front of the house a few nights ago, I've had them to the vet and they'll be fine. We've been wondering how they got there but assumed someone chucked them out of a vehicle."

Brandy hugged the grey kitten tighter. "Darren got angry and tossed them all in his truck, then he tore off with them and we never saw them again. He said they were gone, and we were scared to ask for details."

Tammy had buried her face in the little black kitten's fur. She looked up. "There was a mother cat and two more babies, did they make it?"

As if on cue the yellow and white kitten emerged from the laundry room and twined around my ankles. "Mew!" I scooped him up. "Just this little guy, Ian saw an adult cat and a kitten on the road the following day. They hadn't survived." I frowned and shook my head.

"Were they grey tabbies?" Brandy asked. When Ian answered in the affirmative, she looked at her mother and said, "I'm sorry about Miss Kitty, momma, I know you loved her."

Tammy's eyes watered with fresh tears, and she hugged the black kitten so tightly it began to squirm.

The kitchen door opened, and Yvonne and my mother came in with several cloth bags full of stuff. Jacob was right behind them, laden with bags of sandwiches from the sub shop and a few Walmart bags.

Ian and Arista sprang to help. Their grandma wouldn't allow anyone to touch her bags. Yvonne explained they had been Christmas shopping, and the contents were top secret.

I set kitty on the floor and helped Jacob unload the

food on the counter. "Wow, you went to Walmart? That explains why it took a while for you to get here. I'd started to worry."

"I knew you hadn't made it to the store, and we were about out of cream for the coffee." Jacob grinned. "Besides, I figured we could use some stuff to go with the sandwiches."

The next several minutes were filled with bustling around the kitchen, setting the food out and getting plates, napkins, and silverware. We don't use plastic utensils, ever, because of the negative impact on the environment.

Tammy watched the activity, which could be described as organized chaos, with an astonished expression. "Wow, is it always this busy around here?" she asked.

I laughed. "You caught us on a slow night, there are only three teenagers here tonight."

During supper Lester regaled Tammy with stories of Jacob, our older sister and me as children. We would show up down at the Duke household to mooch cookies and play with their Chihuahuas. Lester had the one Chi left, Violet, and his beloved wife was in the nursing home after a stroke left her unable to do for herself.

Ian and Jacob bantered about video games and techy stuff and by the end of the meal Tammy was relaxed enough to giggle at the antics.

Arista finished eating and got up to clear dishes from the table. "Brandy, are you ready for the biology test tomorrow? I've got the notes from today's review if you want them."

"Shoot, my book and notes are in my locker, I'd forgotten all about it. I better pass that test, or I will get kicked out of softball before the season even starts." The girls scooped up two kittens and headed for Arista's room.

Ian cleared the plates from his side of the table and excused himself. He was quietly non-committal about how he would spend the rest of the evening. I seriously doubted it would be studying. Yvonne and Mom adjourned to Mom's room, I suspected they were stashing the Christmas presents. Lester asked Jacob to give him a hand in the machine shed, which was a well-lit shop with a concrete floor. Lester had run into issues while he worked on the ATV.

I started putting the few dibs and dabs of salads away in the fridge. Tammy offered to help. "Tonight, you are our guest and absolved of kitchen duty." I tossed the dishrag in the sink, "Come on, it's time for that nickel tour."

I took Tammy through the family room and down the hall to the room I had mentally set aside for her. It was a small bedroom at the end of the hallway on the left, decorated in a sunflower motif. Ian had dropped her bag at the foot of the double bed. I showed her the main bathroom in the hall. "The kids mostly use it so if it is occupied, there is a half bath down this way.

"Wow, your house is beautiful! And so big, how do you clean up all this space?" Tammy asked, looking curiously at the staircase.

I laughed. "You haven't noticed the dust bunnies yet, if they get any larger, I'll have to give them names. Seriously, the kids are a big help. They clean their rooms and are responsible for the main bathroom. We all work together on the family room and the downstairs, but it's easy. The loft bedroom is the only thing upstairs, that's where Jacob stays when he's here, but he finally learned to pick up after himself."

"When he's here? Where is he the rest of the time?" Tammy asked.

I had seen her watching my brother with curiosity earlier. I suspected a crush was developing. *Better find a way to nip that in the bud.* "California," I replied without explanation.

I heard the kitchen door open and close, conversation and giggling. *That should do it.*

Tammy followed me back to the kitchen and her face went white at the sight of Deputy Jana Smith in her uniform. "Deputy, has something else happened?" Tammy stammered.

I wondered if she thought they had changed their mind about letting Brandy go and had come to pick her up.

Jacob put his arms around Jana from behind. Jana giggled and smacked him. "No, Ms. Turner, nothing new, at least not on your cases." Jana turned her attention to me. "I would have been here sooner but after we finished up at her house, the sheriff caught a domestic out on Brindle Road. I went to back him up. Domestic calls can go south fast."

Tammy winced and Jana noticed. I could tell she regretted her word choice. Time to change the subject. "Jana, I bet you're hungry, can I get out some food for ya?"

"I'm starving, you're awesome. I'm gonna grab a quick shower and change first though."

Lester pushed open the kitchen door. "All right you two, clear a path, get a room," he grumbled good naturedly. He then announced he was going to bed and wished us all a good night.

Jana headed through to the stairs and took them two at a time, Jacob was right behind her.

"Would you like a cup of hot chocolate or another coffee, Tammy?" I asked as I got out the milk and poured it in a pan for my hot chocolate. I subtly watched her wheels turning.

"No thank you. So…they're a couple?" She gestured in the direction of Jacob and Jana. She was expecting the answer I was about to give her and mild disappointment showed on her face.

"They are. Jake spends more time here now than he has in years. Silicon Valley may be good for his business, but it lacks a Jana. I'm going in by the fireplace, would you like to join me?"

"If it's all the same to you I'm going to bed. It has been a long day." Tammy stretched and headed out of the kitchen and down the hallway.

I sat on the couch by the fireplace. The flames danced and the coziness soothed my frayed nerves. It had been too warm to warrant keeping a proper fire, but we keep a supply of *cheater logs,* as Daddy used to call them. We use the Duraflame logs and light them for ambiance rather than warmth.

The yellow and white kitten appeared out of nowhere and climbed up onto my lap. "Hi Tiny Bits, where have you been hiding all evening?"

"Merp."

"I guess we found your people. I'm going to miss you if you go home with the Turners."

"Mmrow." The little guy climbed up my chest and head bumped my chin. He sat down and stared at me. I gazed into deep blue eyes and absently wondered if they would change colors like so many kitten eyes do, ending up some shade of hazel/green. "Mew!"

"We'll have to see about that, buddy." He curled up and began to purr. It's astonishing how such a little beast can emit such a loud rumble.

Jana and Jacob thundered down the stairs. "Looks like that kitten has taken up with you, sis."

I started to get up.

Jana waved me off. "Stay there, don't wake the baby. I can get my own food." She smiled and continued to the kitchen.

Jacob sat on the other end of the couch with a thoughtful expression. I waited.

"Fen, are you worried about letting the Turners stay here? There is something going on, not that it is their fault or anything, but Jana told me it was apparent whoever ransacked their house was looking for something."

CHAPTER 16

"I will admit that very thing crossed my mind, but Jacob, they have to stay somewhere. Tammy told me they don't have extra money for a hotel. Heck her car isn't even running, she is having to bum rides to work. We have the room, and it's only for a couple days."

"Yeah, sissy, I know. I've decided not to go back to California until after the New Year. Uncle John asked Jana to postpone her vacation for the time being, so we won't be going skiing. I don't want you and Gram and the twins here by yourselves with everything that is going on. Basically, you're stuck with me for a few weeks."

I laughed, "Baby bro, this is your home, too. You don't ever need to make excuses to be here or apologize for your presence. I rather like having you around, but don't let that go to your head. What about your business though, can they get along without you for that length of time?"

Jacob grinned. "That's the awesome part of being the boss, besides as long as we keep the WIFI on I can work fine from here. By the way, would you have any objection to me adding some furniture to the loft room?"

I shook my head. "Not at all, do as ye will, brother."

Jacob went to the kitchen to hang out with Jana, and I scooped up my kitten and went to bed. *My kitten. Feels right. Hope the Turners have no objection.*

A montage of scenes from the last several days haunted my dreams. *Kittens in the road, bodies, bale spikes, a motor home in flames. The Turners' little house tossed about like a ship on high seas. A dumpster brimming with blood and bodies and a shadowy figure laughing.*

I woke up sweating. "Geez Fen, you're turning exaggeration into an art form, a dumpster full of blood indeed. There wasn't that much blood." I grumbled to myself. I must have been tossing and turning, both cats, little and large were curled on the far corner of the bed, away from my feet. The ample moonlight streaming in my window illuminated two pairs of eyes glaring at me. "I'm sorry, don't look at me like that."

I checked my phone, 2:00 a.m. *Damn it.* I sighed and rejected the thought of getting up and getting on with my day. I pulled up the list of meditations I kept on my iPad, scrolled to my favorite one for sleep and pressed *Play.* I rolled over and smacked my pillow into shape.

Moments later there was movement at the foot of the bed. A heavy weight landed on my feet, a tiny "Mew" sounded and a much lighter weight curled up in my hair against the back of my head. I drifted off to sleep listening to the combination of spa music and rumbling purrs.

The six a.m. alarm was most unwelcome. I hit the snooze button. Ten minutes later I silenced the blaring thing again, remembered there were extra people in the house and wrenched myself out of bed. Little kitty stretched and rolled around on his back, wallowing in the covers and yawning. Isabella gave me the stink eye and went back to sleep. *I would like to be a cat in my next life, please.*

I decided to grab a quick shower first and was fully dressed for the day when I hit the kitchen twenty minutes later. Lester drank coffee at the island. I flipped the oven onto 375 degrees and grabbed my favorite coffee mug.

Lester watched me over the rim of his mug. "G'mornin."

"Hey."

"Rough night?" he asked.

"Yep, you?"

"Not too good," he said. "I've got that doctor's appointment today."

I took a long drink of coffee and let the hot liquid burn down my throat. It was heavenly. "Are you worried about it?"

"Nah, I just want to get it over with. What are ya' makin' for breakfast?" Lester asked.

"Jacob got one of those huge, premade breakfast pizzas last night." I retrieved it from the fridge and freed it from the packaging. It was larger than any pan in my kitchen so onto the rack it went. "We'll see what it's like."

"Farm eggs are better." Lester poured more coffee into his cup.

"I know, the chickens are laying fewer eggs right now, I think they are molting their feathers. Besides, we are completely out of bacon, sausage and ham. I hope to get to the store today."

"Have you considered raising a pig or two for the freezer like your daddy used to do?" Lester asked.

"I never liked raising pigs. I don't trust them, but yes, I have considered it and rejected the idea. Although it would be nice to have a freezer full," I replied and sipped my coffee.

Lester nodded and we sat in companionable silence for several minutes. There was a light scratching at the door and I opened it so two small, somewhat damp dogs could run in, shake and tear off through the house.

"Did it rain last night?" I asked.

"No, we had a heavy dew. Supposed to rain later though. This nice weather ain't gonna last forever," Lester declared.

The oven timer dinged, and I removed the pizza, plopped it on its dismantled box and cut it into awkward slices. It didn't look like much, but it smelled okay.

As if on cue, Ian strolled in with his backpack and spied the pizza. "Cool!" He reached for a piece.

"That's hot, get a plate," I said.

He complied. "Ouch, it is hot, mmm, good stuff, thanks, Mom."

Arista and Brandy came in followed by Tammy. Morning greetings were exchanged and I placed a cup of coffee in front of Tammy. She accepted it with a smile. Thanks Fen."

The kids wolfed down their breakfast and sprinted for the bus stop.

Jacob and Jana descended the stairs. Jana was already dressed in her deputy uniform, her hair in a tidy braid. Jacob wore faded jeans and a t-shirt. They helped themselves to coffee and breakfast.

"Tammy what is your plan for the day? Do you have to be anywhere?" I asked.

"I called the nursing home to see if I could be off at 4 p.m. so Brandy and I can go talk to Sheriff Peters like he asked. Ruth told me to come and go as needed today. She's a really good boss. I hate to ask, but I kinda need a ride to work."

"No problem, I can drop you off," Jana said. "How long before you are ready to go?"

"I can be ready in five minutes, thank you, Deputy," Tammy replied. I saw a flash of disappointment in her eyes, but I didn't think anyone else noticed.

"Tammy, what's wrong with your car?" Lester asked.

"It won't stay running. It would start and sputter then die. I did that too many times and I think I killed the battery," Tammy said sheepishly.

Lester and Jacob shared a look and said, "Fuel filter," simultaneously. Then they launched into a discussion about what else it could be if it wasn't that.

"If you want to leave us your keys, we can go get it with the trailer, bring it back here and work on it." Lester told Tammy.

There was some verbal wrestling about that being too much trouble and so on, but in the end, Tammy relented and gave her car keys to Lester.

Jana and Tammy left. Jacob and Lester were about to leave, too. "Lester, where are you guys going? What about your doctor appointment this morning?" I asked.

"We're going to get her car, it's only a couple miles away, won't take long. The appointment is at 10 a.m." Lester shrugged into his jacket.

I watched them go. The house became quiet. Mom and Yvonne were likely still asleep. We recently acquired a daybed with a thick memory foam mattress and placed it in Mom's suite for when Yvonne wanted to stay over. She reported it was way more comfortable than her bed at home. What she didn't say was that her house felt lonely since her husband passed last year. I was happy to have her here as much as she wanted, it was good companionship for Momma, and it helped ensure she wasn't left alone for long periods of time.

I practically ran to my jewelry studio downstairs; I hadn't had a peaceful moment for days and I intended to make the most of an almost empty house.

I emerged from my studio an hour and a half later feeling refreshed. Lester was in the kitchen trying to wash his greasy good hand with the hand in a cast. It wasn't going well and he appeared frustrated. "Would you like some help?" I asked.

"I would like this consarn cast off my arm!" he growled. "I'm sorry, that was rude. No, I 'bout got it."

"I understand. I'm ready to leave whenever you are. Where's Jake?"

"He's still tinkering on the car. I'm ready to go."

We headed into town, and I dropped Lester off at his doctor's office with five minutes to spare. I'd pulled into the parking lot at the local Walmart when my phone rang and roared. I groaned. *Simultaneous calls and texts are never a good sign.* A horn blared behind me. I pulled into the nearest spot to get out of the way and reached for my phone.

The caller ID showed the school was calling. My inner alarm bells went crazy and any vestige of calm I'd achieved in my jewelry studio was gone in a flash. "Hello."

"Mrs. Stern?" a female voice on the phone asked.

I recognized her to be Renata, the school secretary. "Yes, are my kids okay?" My voice did not disguise my panic.

CHAPTER 17

"This is Renata, up at the school. Yes, your kids are fine, but we need you up here. Arista has been in a fight and Principal Snodgrass needs to see you."

There were voices in the background, the calm one sounded like Principal Snodgrass. I was sure the other voice was that awful Vanderkamp woman. *Oh no!*

"I'll be right there, Renata, I'm already in town."

I quickly checked the text messages for clues to this new drama. There were two:

Arista, "Mom, need you at school, now"

Ian, "Sis broke some guy's nose better get here."

I peeled out of the parking lot and raced to the school. Sheriff Peters was pulling out of the convenience store as I went by, he flipped his lights and bleeped his siren at me as a warning to slow down. I waved and went on.

I pulled into a spot in the visitor parking area at the high school and dashed to the double doors. There is a button you must push in order to alert staff of your presence. I bounced from one foot to the other impatiently until they buzzed me in.

Principal Snodgrass' office is within the block of administrative offices to the right as you enter the main door. Renata met me at the main door to administration and ushered me in.

She whispered, "Vanderkamp is pushing for expulsion. Snodgrass is on your side but has to do something. The kid she smacked is a Junior and had it coming."

Renata had been the school secretary since Jacob and I went to school there. She'd seen her share of all manner of teenage drama. She had her finger on the pulse of the school.

I quickly digested this intel as she pushed me into the principal's office. Arista sat in a chair on one side of the room. She tapped her foot, her arms were crossed and she looked madder than a rabid badger.

On the other side of the room was a rather scruffy looking male, who held an icebag to his nose.

Principal Snodgrass extended his hand to shake. "Fenreya, thank you for coming. There has been a dust up between Arista and Duane Jones."

"Mrs. Stern, your daughter attacked Duane in the hallway," screeched Vanderkamp.

This brought Arista to her feet. "I did not! He was saying terrible stuff to Brandy and then he *PUSHED* her up against the lockers! *Then* he put his hands on me."

"Miss Stern, sit down this instant and shut your mouth. I am speaking to your mother," Vanderkamp growled.

"Now ladies—" began Principal Snodgrass but he was cut off by Duane.

"Yeah, no. I was just talking to that little bitch that kilt my Uncle Darren and that one clocked me from behind." Duane pointed at Arista.

My wheels were churning through my internal compendium of local news. *Duane Jones, of our district championship winning football team, linebacker, I think. He's related to McNamara. Vanderkamp has issues with me and is taking it out on my daughter. A picture from the local newspaper popped to mind. The mayor, head football coach and Vanderkamp with a headline about how securing the district championship was good for the local economy.*

"That's enough Duane, you will wait your turn to speak. Clean up your language, too," said the principal.

Vanderkamp glared at me with an air of superiority. I took a deep breath and waded in. Out of deference to our long-time principal I included him in my missive, but I looked Vanderkamp directly in the eye. "Principal Snodgrass knows that my daughter is not a violent person. I will tell you, Ms. Vanderkamp, that Arista has been raised to defend herself and others who are in harm's way, that violence is a last resort and under no circumstances is she to allow herself to be victimized.

"Furthermore, your assertion that a varsity linebacker on your football team was injured in any meaningful way by a freshman is ludicrous and if his claim of getting *clocked from behind* is to be believed, why is his nose bleeding?" I paused in case there was an intelligent reply coming.

Vanderkamp stared at me, arms crossed tightly across her chest. "Nevertheless, Ms. Stern, our district has a zero-tolerance policy when it comes to physical violence. I will be recommending your daughter be expelled immediately."

I turned my gaze to Principal Snodgrass and then to Arista. "Arista, is it true that Duane pushed Brandy up against the lockers? Then subsequently put his hands on you?"

"Yes, ma'am."

"Principal Snodgrass, would it be fair to say that Duane is over six feet tall and what, maybe 210 pounds?"

"I'm 6'1" and go 215." Duane stood to his full height and puffed up his chest.

Principal Snodgrass shrugged and nodded. The glimmer in his eyes told me he knew where I was going with this.

"So, Superintendent Vanderkamp, may I assume that you will be expelling Duane as well, since a huge, older, male student shoving freshman girls around most certainly counts as *physical violence*?" I glanced over at Duane, who appeared gob smacked. "Bummer about your football career." I returned my attention to Vanderkamp. *Checkmate.* I waited.

Principal Snodgrass hid a smile behind a cough and Arista didn't bother hiding her smile at all. She enjoyed watching Momma work.

Superintendent Vanderkamp narrowed her eyes, the notion that she was beaten at her own game began to sink in. She uncrossed her arms and fiddled with a knickknack on the corner of the principal's desk. When she raised her eyes back to me, they were full of hatred but her voice remained calm.

"You make a good point, Ms. Stern, expelling two bright, engaging students over an unfortunate bit of teenage melodrama hardly serves the greater good.

Three days suspension for each of them and they will be allowed to make up any midterm exams that they've missed."

I hadn't thought of that. Good deal.

I glanced at Arista, her expression told me she was still mad but found the proposed punishment acceptable. I tilted my head and peered at Vanderkamp to let her know I was considering our options.

"We will accept those terms." I turned to Principal Snodgrass and shook his hand again. "Thank you for all you do for the school, Principal. Would you have Renata email me a copy of the school incident report and disciplinary action sheet? Oh, and I trust that the school nurse has documented the extent of the alleged injury?"

"You know she did, and I most certainly will, Fen, thanks for coming in and I'm sorry for the trouble," he said warmly.

I nodded, "Come on Arista, we're leaving." I gave my daughter a look that meant *Not a word, be polite.*

Arista got up and preceded me out the office door. Once we were out in the hallway, she hugged me. "Mom, that was awesome. You handed that woman her, um, butt."

"Shoosh you, wait till we get in the truck. Text your brother, he's beside himself."

I checked my phone, there was a text from Lester. He was done at the doctor's office and wondered where I was. *Oh dear, I'd forgotten about him.* I shot a quick text back that read, "Long story, on my way."

We pulled into the clinic parking lot. Lester waited outside. His arm was conspicuously missing the cast and he was smiling. I told Arista to hop in the backseat so he could sit in front.

"Hi, Arista, are you sick? Why aren't you in school?" Lester's smile faded to an expression of concern.

"Oh, I'm fine, I punched a jerk at school and mom had to come up there. He totally deserved it, but now I'm suspended. Hey, you got your cast off!" Arista smiled.

If Lester was stunned by this information, he didn't show it. "Yep, what a relief it is!" He rubbed his arm and stretched it out.

I put the truck in gear and pulled to the lot exit. "I'm sorry you had to wait on me. The issue at the school held me up, I never made it to the grocery store."

"No worries, you know how doctors are, I spent most of the time waiting in their little room. I'd jus' been out a few minutes. Can I buy you ladies lunch? I feel like celebrating and I want Cashew Chicken."

Instead of turning right for the store I turned left for our local Asian restaurant. There was only one and they would have their lunch buffet up and running. "Sounds good, Lester, thanks I could smash some Sesame Chicken." A glance in the rearview mirror told me that Arista wasn't listening, she was texting.

The three of us walked into the Rusty Dragon, named for its large dragon statue, which was indeed rusty, and grabbed a table in the middle of the room as all the booths were full. The buffet table steamed and smelled great. I realized how famished I'd become. *Probably good that grocery shopping was delayed.*

Never shop when you're hungry.

We were well into our first plates full of food when Jacob and Jana walked in. "Hey, fancy meeting y'all here!" Greetings were exchanged all around and they scooted an adjacent table over and joined us.

Jacob surveyed the table and met my eyes. Rather than ask why Arista wasn't in school he asked, "Where's Ian?"

I'd noticed Rebecca, noted local gossip extraordinaire from the feed store, at the counter picking up a to-go order. I shook my head. "He is in school, I'll fill you in later." I was attempting to keep our family business out of the rumor mill.

Arista, on the other hand, began the tale. I kicked her under the table and shook my head again. "Ouch! Mom! Oh." She took the hint and resumed eating her lunch. Jana laughed.

Lester changed the subject, "Jake, how'd it go on that old car? Is it gonna make it?"

Jacob swallowed his bite. "I am cautiously optimistic. That's why I'm in town. I came in to grab a fuel filter and some new plugs and plug wires."

"And here I thought you came to see me!" Jana teased.

The rest of the meal was ripe with friendly banter and when we were all full, we filed out into the parking lot. Jana kissed my brother goodbye and left in her *deputy mobile* as we'd taken to calling her sheriff's department truck. Lester elected to ride home with Jacob so they could finish fixing Tammy's little car.

When Arista and I climbed into the truck, my intention was to go grab some groceries. Both our phones went off with text notifications. One text from

Tammy said, "Hey sorry to bother you, Brandy and I need a ride to the sheriff's department for a 4 p.m. meeting."

I sent back, "K, pick you up at 3:30." I would go get Tammy then head over to the school, since they let the kids out at 3:45.

Arista read her message. "Ian wants to know if we can pick him up from school. He feels left out, I think." She rolled her eyes.

"Tell him to be outside with Brandy after school. We will pick them both up."

I was recalculating what to get at the store. It was already two o'clock or so and there wasn't enough time to shop, take everything home, put it away and get back to town. *Non-perishables only then. Maybe some frozen sausage.* I sighed.

Ninety minutes and a hundred dollars later, Arista and I pulled up to the nursing home with seven bags of groceries tucked into the bed of the truck. Tammy came out and got into the front seat. "Thank you for picking me up, I hated to ask."

"No problem at all," I replied. We picked up Brandy and Ian as planned and then drove to the sheriff's office and let Brandy and Tammy out. "Tammy, text me when you're done here, and I will be back to pick you up." *Geez, the logistics of this situation is getting complicated.*

I watched them walk into the station and turned to my kids. Arista was telling Ian about her altercation with Duane the linebacker, Ian laughed.

My decision made, I pulled onto the road. *Might as well knock out the run to the feed store.*

Our local feed store was a hub of local information.

Rebecca worked the desk and ran the office. Seeing her at the restaurant earlier reminded me that we were out of cattle feed. *I might as well grab chicken feed too. If I stock up, I can avoid coming back until after New Years.*

I told the kids to move the groceries to the truck cab and wait there. I went inside. Rebecca greeted me cheerfully.

"Hey Fen, saw y'all at the diner, their food is always so good. I heard Arista had a little dust up at school, is she okay?"

Wow, that was fast. She's fishing though.

"Oh sure, she's fine, no worries." I smiled and read through the list of feeds hanging on the wall. *Wonder if I should grab some mineral blocks.*

"Duane's granny came in here to pick up dogfood, they raise those little, long dogs, when she got the call from her daughter, which would be Duane's momma, tellin' her that he got attacked by the Stern girl," she paused.

I waited for her to go on. I knew this game and wouldn't lay my cards down until she showed me hers. *I might as well spin this in a better direction.*

Rebecca continued, "That all sounded like hogwash to me, Arista jus' ain't that way."

"You are so right, Rebecca, she isn't one to go around attacking anyone, certainly not football players who outweigh her by a hundred pounds. My daughter has brass but she's not stupid.

"See, what happened was he got a little fresh with her and one of her friends and she slapped him." I lowered my voice like the whole thing was a scandal. I knew Rebecca would not be able to resist this version of events.

"See, I figured it was something like that. I heard Duane fancies himself a ladies' man but that he ain't too bright. So, what can I get ya today?" Rebecca said, switching gears.

I gave her our feed order, grabbed my load ticket, and walked out to the warehouse dock. Since the arrest of their old dock worker, Denny Bowman, last month, the feed store was short-handed, and I had to wait for several minutes for the guy to get our order together.

Once the truck was loaded, we hit the road for home. I felt anxious to get the feed home before it started raining, which was imminent judging by the sky.

It was already starting to spatter rain on the windshield when we got home so I pulled all the way into the barn, grabbed most of the groceries and trotted to the house. I left the kids to unload the feed and move the truck once they were done. I saw Jacob and Lester over by the machine shop, the garage style door open, with Tammy's little car parked inside. It was running, although it sounded kinda rough.

It was nice to be home. I found a note on the kitchen island from Yvonne. She and Mom went to the senior center for movie night and they would be eating there, back by nine p.m.

I fixed myself a cup of coffee and mentally counted noses. How many people would I need to feed tonight? I came up with eight. Hmm. The last time I made stew, it was a triple batch and there were two gallon-sized containers in the freezer. *Wish I'd thought to pull those out this morning. Oh well.*

I'm not a huge fan of microwaves and the containers wouldn't fit anyway, so I grabbed my enameled roaster and emptied the containers into it. The stew popped right out like big, beefy ice cubes. I added a bit of water and popped it in the oven, cranking it up to 400 degrees. *Problem solved.*

The kids, Jacob, and Lester all burst through the kitchen door. The kids put the remaining groceries on the counter and left the kitchen. Jacob and Lester washed their grimy hands at the kitchen sink. "We got the little car running!" Lester's voice sounded triumphant.

"That's wonderful, well done!"

"I got a text from Jana, she is going to bring Tammy and Brandy with her, so no one has to go pick them up." Jacob peeked in the oven. "Mmm, stew."

"Also, wonderful. I am truly tired of driving for today." I sighed and got out the ingredients for cornbread. Since I didn't have to leave the house, I had time to whip up a batch to go with the stew. I would wait to bake it until the stew was hot. The timer on my phone would serve as a reminder.

"I'll be in my studio guys," I said over my shoulder as I left the kitchen and headed downstairs.

It seemed like no time at all passed before my phone dinged. I trudged back upstairs and into the kitchen. Tammy stood in the kitchen talking with Lester about her car. I figured Brandy was with Arista and Jana was likely with Jacob. I stirred the stew, saw that it was hot and popped the pan of cornbread in the oven.

"Hi, Tammy, how did it go at the meeting with the sheriff?" I asked.

"It went okay, I guess, neither of us got arrested." She chuckled. "The sheriff asked some strange questions though. I didn't really know the answers. He interviewed us separately and Brandy's lawyer went in with her. He seems like a nice guy."

"Was it the young public defender? I forget his name," I said, and when she nodded, I continued, "I haven't met him. What kind of strange questions did Sheriff Peters ask?"

"He wanted to know all about Darren, what he did for money, where he spent his time, who he hung out with. That all seemed normal. Then he wanted to know if Darren owned any property or other vehicles besides his old truck and if he had a storage unit anywhere. He asked a lot of stuff about our house and the break-in, had Darren come into any money recently, stuff like that." Tammy stopped talking and fidgeted with a thread dangling from her sleeve.

"Were you able to answer any of those questions?" I probed. I wanted as many answers as I could get, why couldn't she just spill it without me having to politely dig for it.

"Oh, Darren kept me out of his business. I'd only met a couple of his friends, and if he had any money or anything like that he never let on." Tammy bit the thread off and tossed it in the trash. "The sheriff said we could go back home by Saturday as long as nothing else goes haywire. Can I help you with anything around here?"

"You can set the table if you want, eight places should do it, then holler at everyone and tell them supper is ready."

I pointed out where the dishes and so forth were kept

and began to shuttle food to the table.

Later, after supper was over and the table cleared, I intended to go back to my jewelry studio and finish the bracelet I started for Merry, my older sister. There was no rush, she wouldn't be home for Christmas, and even if I mailed it tomorrow the package wouldn't arrive in France in time for the holiday.

I heard activity in the den and went to investigate. Arista, Ian and Brandy were in there, standing around the whiteboard on the wall. "Hey, whatcha doin'?"

"We are making a *murder board* like they do on TV," Arista said proudly.

CHAPTER 18

Great. The kids have caught Jessica Fletcheritis. "Is that so?"

"Yep, check it out."

Ian pointed to the board. Across the top he'd written, *Victims* and that was divided into three columns *RV Guy, McNamara, and Dumpster Guy.* Underneath that were rows for *Known Associates, Murder Weapon, and Suspects.*

My curiosity piqued, and I walked further into the room. Studying the board, I noticed that most of it remained blank, we really didn't know all that much.

The map that we used last month to plot the locations of the cattle thefts was still tacked to the wall to the left of the whiteboard.

"How about we plot the locations where the victims were found on the map?" I suggested. I put a tack at the site of the RV fire where RV Guy was found, Ian plotted the sites of the other bodies. We all stepped back and stared at the map and the whiteboard as if waiting for some grand *Ahha* moment to occur. It didn't. A couple of us sighed.

Jana walked in with Jacob right behind her. Jana said, "Hey what's that?"

Jacob shook his head. "Oh, you have got to be kidding me."

"It's a murder board and a map with the crime scenes plotted on it," Brandy explained.

Jana gazed thoughtfully at the map and adjacent whiteboard. "You're missing one."

My heart skipped a beat. "Missing one what? Another victim?"

Jana swept her hand around the entire room and everyone in it. "Everything said in this room stays in this room. Understand?" Once she received affirmative responses from all the kids she stepped up to the whiteboard and added a fourth column to the victims list. "*Missing Finger Guy* is technically missing, all we have is a finger."

"Oh, my stars! I never did get the details on what happened there. Was that the incident over by Pine Street? What happened?" I asked.

Jana answered, "I'm not able to tell you all the details. The sheriff would wring my neck. But basically a lady's dog brought home a human finger. We don't know exactly where the dog found it. No body or other parts have been recovered. It has been sent to the State Crime Lab for a series of tests. The fingerprints were not on file."

My brain raced to connect the dots. "So, if fingerprints could be checked, that means the skin was largely intact as opposed to skeletal remains." I watched Jana's face for signs.

Seeing none, but remembering my brother's aversion

to all things dismembery, I chose my words carefully and pressed on. "That all would indicate the finger was recently removed from the subject." I glanced over at Jacob, he was quite pale.

"Was it a large finger?" I asked Jana.

"I'll be back a little later." Jake rushed out of the room. *Bless him.*

"Actually, it was kinda big now that I'm thinking about it. Due to damage to the skin, we weren't able to obtain a very good print sample. The partial print we were able to obtain didn't show up in the database. The state lab is going to develop a victim profile based on various biometric measurements and stuff so we will eventually get more details. My off -the- cuff."

There were groans around the room and Jana said, "Sorry, no pun intended. My best guess, based solely on observation, is it came from a larger man with light brown or olive skin."

I wrote *Missing Finger Guy* under the known associates for Dumpster Guy, then I explained, "The two guys I saw Saturday morning talking to McNamara were both dark olive skinned. They dressed like out-of-towners and spoke at least some Spanish. One of the guys was very large, in a thick, muscled meaty kind of way. The other guy was smaller, lean but not skinny or frail. So, if Missing Finger Guy is the associate of Dumpster Guy, they both knew McNamara." The kids were gaping at me with confused expressions.

Jana picked up the thread. "Essentially, these two guys could have killed McNamara but then what? Did the big guy kill the little guy and toss him in the dumpster, but somehow big guy lost his finger in the process? We need a timeline."

Tammy stuck her head in the room. "Brandy, I was wondering where you were, come talk to me. We need to figure some things out."

Jacob returned. "Has the subject changed back to plain old murder yet?"

"Yep, come on back, bro. Sorry about earlier, I was trying to find words that wouldn't trigger you, weren't any."

"It's all good, sissy." Jacob peered at the board and the newly added timeline. "Hmm, looks like progress. Where is the car those goons were driving?"

"That's a great question, we didn't have enough information to put out a BOLO. Presumably, this guy, (she pointed at Missing Finger Guy) drove off in it," Jana said.

Jacob nodded. "Okay, so what is the motive? What links these guys together?"

Arista piped up and held up two fingers. "Drugs or maybe money, but I'm betting on drugs."

"Yes, but what about them? Drugs are bad, yes, but the sheer presence of drugs in a given situation doesn't morph people into murderers." We all gaped at Jacob. "Hear me out. There should be a bigger motive. This is hard to explain. Where are the drugs that we think are the motive for all this violence? Show me the double cross. Who stole them from whom, who has them now, were they the reason the Turner's house was ransacked?"

Jana was nodding, the kids looked utterly confused, but I was beginning to catch on.

Jana spoke first. "These three guys are dead." She drew an "X" over their column headings. "And this guy," she circled *Missing Finger Guy*, "is in the wind.

Unless he is the one guy that is responsible for this mess and just happened to lose his finger along the way, there is another player. At least one, maybe more."

The reality of her words slammed into me. I remembered the shadowy figure in my dream, laughing in the background. I felt the color drain from my face and sat heavily down on the arm of the chair Arista sat in.

They were all peering at me, but it was Jacob who spoke.

"Are you okay, Fen?"

"Yeah, I'm okay. And while all this is fascinating, it's giving me a headache plus it is time for you kids to be in bed."

"I am off school tomorrow," Arista said.

"Being suspended is not the same as being off, you will keep your regular bedtime, and tomorrow you will get up and help with the house."

"Yes, ma'am." The kids slouched off to their rooms.

Jacob and Jana were staring and Jana said, "What set you back, really?"

"You will think it's crazy." I prefaced and told them about my dream and the laughing mystery man.

"After the events of last month, I'm willing to take pretty much anything you say at face value. So, no I don't think you are crazy. Sadly, unless you can dream a picture of the guy in a mugshot with his name and all, none of that helps close this case." Jana smiled sardonically.

I shook my head and laughed. "I'll see what I can do."

Jacob chuckled. "I think you're both kinda nuts."

To which we replied in stereo, "We didn't ask you."

Jacob and Jana went downstairs to play some billiards. I'd heard Yvonne come in with Mom earlier and went to check on them. Mom was already asleep. Yvonne was propped up reading and appeared to be staying. She reported they had a good time, the old movie was as good as ever, but everyone had seen it and spent most of the evening reminiscing about when, where and with whom. I said goodnight and pulled the door partly closed behind me.

I headed into the kitchen to ensure no burners were on and the oven was off. I made sure the door was locked.

"Hey kitten, where are you?" I hadn't seen the little guy in hours. I heard a tiny thump. "Mew!" He scampered to me and stopped at my feet. "Hi, Bitsy, ready for bed?"

"Mrerp."

"Aw, you're such a good baby."

When the six a.m. alarm went off, I got up. I slept remarkably well in spite of all the stressful, strange events happening. I felt grateful for the rest.

The dogs met me by the kitchen door, and I let them out to go potty. A faint glow on the eastern horizon claimed the sun was trying to come up and peek out from behind thinning clouds. The weather guru thought the second round of rain would miss us. *Yeah, we'll see.*

I stirred cream into my coffee, no sign of Lester but the coffee didn't make itself. *He must be in the shower.* I took my coffee back to my room and enjoyed reading uninterrupted for a whole 30 minutes.

My next foray into the kitchen found it full of people. Lester, Jana, Jacob and Tammy were drinking coffee and chatting. Tammy seemed excited at the prospect of being able to drive herself to work now that her little car was running. Jana offered to follow her in, to be on the safe side.

"What, you don't have any faith in my, um, our, mechanical abilities?" Jacob wore an expression of mock hurt on his face. Lester played along.

"Oh no, I have total faith in y'all, it's motorized vehicles in general that I don't trust." Jana flung an arm around Jake's shoulders. *Good save.*

"I agree, my momma always said if it had tires or testicles, it was gonna be trouble!" Tammy laughed then added, "No offense fellas."

Brandy and Ian went to meet the bus. Tammy left and Jana followed behind her. Jacob returned to the loft to do whatever Jacob does before nine a.m. Lester went out to putter in the machine shop.

I indulged in a third cup of coffee at the kitchen island. I felt I missed something. I checked my calendar. There was an entry for today. It read Dogs/monthly bug pills. *Pretty straightforward.* I went in the laundry room, where a large counter with built-in drawers below and cabinets above housed all pet medicines not requiring refrigeration. I dug through the cabinet twice. We were out of the meds that protect the dogs from fleas, worms etc. *Great, I planned to stay home today. Huh, I'm going to the vet clinic to pick up meds. Might not be too bad.* I brightened at the thought and went to my room to clean up.

About an hour later, clad in nice jeans, a burgundy

V-neck sweater with a wire-wrapped Rose Quartz pendant on a silver chain, I hopped in my truck and headed for town.

On the way I considered the possibility I was interested in Dr. Will Spencer. I dismissed the notion. *What a silly idea, I'm married. Am I? It's been ten years.* I also considered I should finish the grocery shopping I didn't get done yesterday. It made more sense even though it didn't sound very fun.

I sighed and turned on the radio. A song came on called *Thinking of You* or something like that. I am terrible at knowing the names of songs and artists. This was a beautiful song and the singer's voice was deep, melodious and sexy. However, it wasn't at all helpful for my current state of mind. I changed the channel to classic rock. Twilight Zone by Golden Earring came on. I turned it up and sang along to drown out thoughts of cute vets, missing husbands and a few hundred dollars of groceries. It could all wait.

I pulled into the parking lot at the veterinary clinic and parked in front. My phone roared with a text. *Now what?* The message was from Auntie Lou, it stated, "Remember, eyes open, choose wisely." *Yes Auntie.* I walked into the clinic.

Julie, the receptionist, sat at the desk as usual. I told her what I needed, and she looked in our file to make sure they had the pills in stock. The door to the back opened and a very large man walked out. He carried a very large dog. The very large dog had a cast on his right front leg and sutures along his face, his torso was wrapped as well. The very large man was also covered in abrasions. He had a black eye and the knuckles of his left hand were raw and bruised.

Dr. Spencer followed the man out the door and part way into the waiting room. I heard him say, "Jasper was lucky that his lung wasn't punctured, he needs more rest, but he should be okay. Keep watching for signs of infection around the stitches in his face. We should be able to remove the cast in a couple weeks. I wish you would reconsider filing a report—"

The very large man cut off doc's words.

"No, nothing good would come of that." He turned away from the doc and approached the desk.

Doctor Spencer hadn't seen me, he went back into the rear of the building, letting the door close behind him. I was surprised at the disappointment I felt.

Very large man was talking with Julie.

"Yeah, I get paid tomorrow and I can bring up some more money."

Julie said it would be fine although her facial expression told a different story, but what are ya going to do?

I absently wondered if this was the same guy who called about a beaten dog the day I'd brought the kittens in here. I approached the big guy. "Aww poor guy, what happened to him?"

The man grunted something that sounded like "Car accident."

My peripheral vision caught Julie looking up sharply with an unreadable expression on her face.

I pressed on, "Gosh, your poor eye! Were you in the wreck too?" I let the question hang.

The man clenched his jaw. "No, yeah, look it don't matter."

"Goodness, it looks bad, you should get that looked at."

He snorted and headed for the door. I ran after him, "Oh, here, let me get the door for you. Your hands are full." Mostly I wanted to get a look at the vehicle he was getting into. It was the only other one in the parking lot besides mine, but I'd paid zero attention to it when I pulled in.

The big guy gently placed his dog in the back seat of a blue Toyota Corolla, wedged himself into the driver's seat, and sped away. I didn't know why I thought it was important, but I jotted the license plate number down anyway.

I went back inside the clinic to finish my transaction. Julie had put my dog meds in a little bag with my name on it. A receipt showing she had placed it on our account was stapled to the bag.

Doctor Spencer leaned on the reception desk. He'd watched my interaction with the very large man. I was suddenly flustered.

"Hi, Dr. Spencer, fancy seeing you here." *Omg, Fen that was dumb.*

He laughed. "I work here, what's your excuse?"

"Just picking up dog meds, where's Julie?" I picked up the little bag and gave it a shake.

"She stepped away for a moment, did you need something else? I will try to help you unless it's about billing. She forbids me to mess with billing. I'm totally okay with that." He laughed.

Wow, he has a real nice laugh, I want to hear more of it. Stop that. "Oh, no, I have everything I need, thanks anyway." I turned to leave. Slowly.

"Fen, do you know that guy that just left? Are you friends?" Dr. Spencer asked.

"No, he looks familiar, but I don't know him, why?"

Doc offered a smile. "I was only wondering. He didn't, I mean, um. He's kind of an odd sort, odd in a dark way and you were so nice to him." Will cast his eyes about the office.

Was he concerned or jealous? He's looking for a reason to stop talking or at least change the subject.

"So, what happened to that poor dog?" I asked.

"He claimed his dog got beat up but refused to share any details. I encouraged him to make a police report, but he didn't want to. One of several odd things about him." Doc shook his head.

"Wow, that is strange. Did you notice the guy was beat up too?"

"Yes, and that's the other thing, he didn't appear to have a scratch on him the other day when he brought the dog in but, today he was a mess."

There was an awkward silence. I thought I'd wrung all the information about the peculiar man out of doc, and continued questioning would make me seem like the odd one.

"Okay, it was good seeing ya, doc, enjoy your day!" I started for the door.

"Um, Fen, I was wondering," Will said.

I froze momentarily. I forced my face to be inscrutable before I turned to face him. I raised my eyebrows in a question because I didn't trust my voice right then.

Will fidgeted and looked kinda miserable, it was adorable. "I was wondering if you'd go to dinner with me sometime soon."

Wanting to hear the words and actually hearing the words are two entirely different things. I was dumbfounded. I finally managed a smile and mumbled,

"That sounds nice, I'll check my calendar and be in touch." I slipped rapidly out the door and into the peace of my truck. I took off so I didn't look like a total lunatic sitting in the parking lot. I went over to Walmart, got as far as the parking lot, and changed my mind. There was food at home, the shopping could wait one more day. There were entirely too many people there, and I was not in a dealing-with-people state of mind. I drove straight home.

CHAPTER 19

I pulled up to the house in my normal spot. BB stood at the fence and snorted a greeting at me when I got out of the truck. I walked over to say a proper hello. "Hey handsome, whatcha doin'?" I patted BB's neck and kissed his soft nose. He knickered softly and head bumped my shoulder gently. "I think we should go riding real soon, before the weather gets nasty again." I whispered it as if telling him a secret. He stomped his foot.

I went into the kitchen and was pleasantly surprised to find the kitchen clean and Arista working in the family room and dining room. She wore earbuds and jammed while she vacuumed. She startled when she saw me standing there.

Arista flipped the switch off on the vacuum. "Hey, Mom, did you see what I got done so far?"

"I did, looks great! Thank you for going to work on it. I'll change clothes and pitch in."

"Sounds good. Also, I was wondering if we could go do something fun, just the two of us? Like maybe tomorrow or Friday?" Arista asked.

"What does my most beautiful daughter have in mind?" I asked.

She giggled and gave the usual response. "I'm your only daughter, Mom. Geez. But I don't care, anything from hiking to going to Springfield, you can choose."

There is that word again. "Choose." Coincidence? "That sounds like a lovely idea, honey, lets both think of a few options and we can decide from there."

Arista seemed happy with my answer and went back to vacuuming. I changed clothes and fretted about everything that happened at the vet's office. I remembered to give the meds to the dogs.

I decided to tackle the laundry. The kids were now responsible for doing their own, but I did the household loads, all of Mom's and my own. Once I had a load going, I turned my attention to supper preparations and briefly wished I'd had the internal fortitude to finish the damn shopping while I was in town. *That was really lame, Fen.*

Arista came in, and I asked her what she thought about breakfast for supper.

"It sounds like an awful lot of work since we have so many people to feed, how about frozen lasagna? There is one of those huge ones in the deep freeze and we have salad stuff."

"Good idea, go get it, will ya, and we'll get it going."

Lester came in around 3 p.m. and poured himself a cup of coffee. He flexed his previously casted arm and winced. "I fixed the side by side, it's running like a top now."

"That's wonderful. Thank you, Lester! What was

wrong with it?" I asked.

His long and detailed answer boiled down to there being gunk in the gas tank which plugged up the fuel filter and fouled the spark plugs. He wiggled his fingers and rubbed them with his other hand.

"So, is your arm and hand bothering you?" I asked, and I started digging for a large basin and my container of Epsom salt.

"Oh, yeah, I guess, but it is better than being broken and casted. I'm hoping it will pass. Before you ask, no, I didn't overdo it working outside."

I took the last bit as defensiveness. Of course he'd overdone it, but I wasn't going to point it out. "How about a nice soak in some herbal Epsom salt water? Any chance you've been doing the exercises I showed you?"

"Uh, not as often as you'd like, I admit. Yeah, I'll soak it if you think it will help." He submerged his arm, in the basin I'd set in front of him, with a sigh.

Brandy got off the bus with Ian and both were full of school gossip to share with Arista. I admit I was curious and hoped to listen, so I put a platter of cookies and a pitcher of tea out on the counter. Arista pumped her brother for information. Ian was more interested in the snacks.

Brandy didn't disappoint though. "Yeah, most everyone was talking about the smackdown. Then at lunch, they let us go outside since it was so nice out. Duane, the Dunce, tried to start up with Ian." She stopped talking and took a bite of cookie. We all looked to Ian to continue the story.

Ian had to swallow his cookie first but managed to mumble, "It was nothing. Duane, the Dunce, thought he could redeem his reputation. He failed." Ian filled his mouth with another cookie.

Arista rolled her eyes at him. I hid a chuckle because I was certain he did it to annoy his sister.

In order to move the story along I said, "Duane, the Dunce? Dunce is an old word, I didn't think kids used it anymore, heck it wasn't even in use when I was in school."

"Its use was resurrected solely for Duane, it totally fits." Arista held up a hand. "I know, you're going to say it's unkind and all that. But, Mom, you saw him. He is obnoxious and dim."

Jacob walked in a moment before and put his two cents in. "Yep, sissy, sometimes the truth hurts. What else did I miss?" He grabbed a glass of tea and drank half of it in one glug.

Brandy spoke up. "Not much, the good part is next. So, Duane got all puffed up in Ian's face and before he could get a word out, Ian is like, 'What's a matter, Duane? Your nose ain't broken enough for ya? You couldn't whoop my sister so you're gonna try me?' But then the science teacher, Mr. Peabody, came outside and broke it up before it even got going. Everyone was laughing though."

Every one of us at the table laughed. I worried we hadn't heard the last of Duane the Dunce and wondered if his issues with my children would come back to haunt them. *He was supposed to be suspended too. That sneaky broad is waiting till after football season. A decision that may come back to bite her.*

Tammy returned from her workday and was smiling for once. "Jacob, Lester, thank you both so much! My little car hasn't run that well in a couple years, it's actually a pleasure to drive it again."

Supper was a pleasant affair, no one brought up murder at all. Once the meal concluded and we started the dishes, Tammy said, "I got some news from the sheriff today. He told me Brandy and I can go home anytime we want. They finished looking for evidence and he had a guy go change the old locks and add a new deadbolt for us. I can pick up the keys tomorrow."

"That's great news, I bet you'll be happy to be back in your own space," I said.

"It's been awesome being here, and I really appreciate y'all taking me and Brandy in. I am kind of anxious to put our house back together and get back to normal, the new normal anyway. I'm gonna go call my momma and tell her everything." Tammy bounced out of the room.

Brandy followed her mom, "Hey I want to talk to Grandma, too!"

I wandered into the family room. Ian and Lester were discussing small engine repair so I left them to it. I checked on my mom, she was ensconced in an episode of NCIS, from season seven, I think, and she was knitting furiously. I'd adopted a theory that during tense, dramatic parts of her show, her knitting speed picked up. I smiled and left her undisturbed. Arista went to her room to play with the kittens and read.

I wanted to do something, but I didn't know what. *If it were light outside, I would take BB out for a ride.* I considered going to my jewelry studio or working out for a while but neither appealed to me then.

Why am I so restless? My phone roared with a text message from Auntie Lou. It read, "You choose the choices before they choose you." *Bugger all, how does she do that?* I replied, "I'm restless Auntie, idk why."

Auntie, "When was the last time you threw some cards?"

Me, "Idk, months?"

Auntie, "Hmm, might try that."

Me, "Where are you? Will u b home for the holidays?"

Auntie, "Key West, FL and yes. Gotta go, Luv u C u."

Me, "Luv u, C u."

That last bit is our own texting shorthand for *Love you, see you,* and we have ended nearly every conversation in that manner since I was very small. We never say "goodbye".

I wandered back to the kitchen during my texting session with Auntie. I started to make a cup of coffee but changed my mind and turned the kettle on for tea.

I scrolled my social media while I waited for the water to boil. I'd immersed myself in the photo feed of a gemstone page until the ambient quiet was broken by a clunk and a prolonged clattering. Something tiny skittered past me, followed by a white and yellow blur. Clunk. I peered around the edge of the counter, the kitten was crouched, ears flattened against his head and the countdown to launch was apparent based on the wiggle.

"What are you doing?" I asked and scooped the kitten up in one hand and reached under the adjacent stool to retrieve the mystery *prey.* I examined the small opaque stone disk. It was a piece of Selenite. I knew exactly where it had come from. I held kitty aloft at eye level. "You naughty little thief, I suppose my tarot cards are all over the floor now." Kitty wiggled and purred. "I'm beginning to think you are in league with Auntie somehow, although I doubt being cooperatively obedient to anyone is in your wheelhouse."

"Mew!"

The teapot began to shriek, announcing the water's vigorous boiling. The sound scared kitty and he leapt from my arms, landed on the counter all puffed up and hissing. I quickly silenced the teapot and scooped the little guy up. "It's okay, Bitsy, just a teapot, you're okay." Kitty eyed the steaming teapot suspiciously and began to wiggle. "You need a proper name, tiny bits." I let the kitten go at my feet so I could fix my tea.

I reached for a calming tea, something with chamomile but out popped a Spicy Hibiscus Raspberry blend. It promised to boost my mood and help me focus all while being naturally caffeine-free. *We'll see about that.* The note on the teabag claimed *your intuition is your friend, your ego is not. Fabulous.*

The family room was empty when I walked through on my way to my bedroom, mug of tea in one hand and kitty cradled in the other arm. I'd carried him since he seemed intent on pouncing on my feet as I walked. It was easier to avoid a spilled tea episode.

I plopped kitty on the bed next to Isabella, whose calico face scrunched into a disapproving scowl. "I know he's a menace, hey maybe his name is Dennis." Isabella swatted the kitten and stalked to the other side of the king-sized bed.

The kitten was unfazed by the smack from Issy and was already off the bed, stirring around in the pile of jumbled tarot cards on the floor at the base of the bookcase. My assumption that kitty spilled them when he captured the Selenite disk was spot on, the fact he'd managed to clear the entire shelf was a surprise. *Geez, glad nothing broke.*

A card popped out of the pile. The kitten batted it across the floor and pounced on it.

"You squirrely little beastie, leave those alone before you tear them up." I picked him up and retrieved the loose card. I gazed at the card. It was *Justice* the Eleventh card in the Major Arcana. *Hmm. Ironic.*

Kitten squirmed to get down and batted at my other hand. "No, you can't have that. My goodness, what a mess you've made." I kissed him on his fluffy little head and dropped him on the bed.

Resigned to the idea the cat, my aunt and evidently the Universe wanted me to consult the tarot about my current state of life, I bent to gather up the rest of the deck. I settled cross legged in the center of my bed and began to shuffle the cards. I have always struggled with formulating a proper question, which is why I haven't used the tarot more often.

I shuffled and sighed. Then an idea hit me. I took a deep breath and closed my eyes.

Guides and Guardians, all about
Gather round and help me out.
Use three cards from this tarot,
Show me what I need to know.

After a few moments when the energy felt right, I drew three cards and laid them face down in a row in front of me. This simple act drew the attention of the cats. Issy, ever the lady, sat down to watch. The kitten attempted to take an active role in the process. I grabbed my journal and put the date at the top of a new page. I turned each card over and made note of the order in which they appeared. Kitty had to be removed a half dozen times. His efforts to help made it difficult to focus on interpretation. I snapped a photo with my phone so I could print it and add it to the journal notes later if I chose. *Maybe I'll send it to Auntie, to prove I followed her advice.*

The first card was the Page of Pentacles. I studied the picture and referred to the little booklet that came with the deck. "Your path is wide open, and you are prepared for new adventures." I looked at the cats. "Hrumpf, I feel like we've all had enough adventures for a while and wish it would settle down."

Isabelle yawned, the kitten pounced on her tail and she smacked him upside the head. Moving on.

Card number two was the Ace of Pentacles. It pictured a woman in a summer setting, surrounded by flowers. She wore a serene expression and held an open packet of seeds in one hand. She appeared to be planting with the other hand. The key words associated with this card were luck, joy, opportunity, and the possibility of good news. I knew from past experience and countless lectures by my auntie that Pentacles involved the Earth Element and physical matters. *Cool, nothing ominous about this card.*

The third card was even more encouraging. The Queen of Wands gazed off in the distance as her dragon friend snorted smoke rings above her head. The description read "This queen channels her passion into glorious, productive forward movement." It also pointed out you can be strong and nurturing at the same time, you don't have to pick one over the other. *Hmm, that sounds vaguely familiar.*

After I made a few notes on the reading, I gathered up the cards and returned them to the shelf. Both cats were asleep. The clock read close to midnight, and I realized how tired I felt. I readied myself for bed and climbed under the blankets. Moments later the world fell away.

CHAPTER 20

Thursday morning was bright and chilly. I dressed in layers and drank coffee at the kitchen island when Lester entered.

"Good morning, Fen, it sure feels good to be driving again. I went and checked my cows, it's a relief to have them home."

"Hey, G'morning. Yes, I'm sure it is a good feeling!"

"I'm going to the nursing home to visit Mary this morning. Does Arista need to go up there or is she suspended from that, too?"

"Good question, I'm not sure, but I don't see any reason for the nursing home to be deprived of their volunteer because of something the school has done."

Arista bounced into the kitchen. "Good morning, y'all. Did I hear my name?"

"Morning, honey. Lester's wondering if you were going to the nursing home today."

"I want to, do you think I should, or is the school going to get mad?"

"They would have to be real jerks to get mad at a young lady for volunteering her time in a nursing home!" Lester declared.

Arista and I rolled our eyes and I said, "Have you met the new superintendent?"

Lester chuckled. "Not officially but I've heard enough stories about her to make me want to avoid her. Arista, I'm heading out in about thirty minutes if you want to ride with me."

Arista glanced at me for permission and saw me nod.

"Yes, please and thank you ,Lester."

I retrieved the hot hashbrown casserole from the oven and placed it on the stove as Ian and his grandma entered the kitchen. The cheese on top was golden brown and still sizzling.

Ian hugged me. "Way cool, I love hash brown casserole!"

Mom peered at the casserole. "Mmm, looks good! Just the way I taught you to make it!"

I beamed at both of them. "Thank you, Mom. You were a good teacher."

Ian put his empty plate in the sink. "Hey Lester, would you mind dropping me off at school on your way to the nursing home?"

Lester sipped his coffee and handed his plate to Ian. "No trouble at all, kiddo. Be ready in ten minutes."

I swallowed the last bite of crispy, cheesy goodness. "Arista, the weather is supposed to be excellent this afternoon. I thought we'd go trail riding. I can have the critters saddled up and loaded, so when I pick you up at the nursing home we can leave from there.

Arista glanced down at her leggings and tennis shoes. "That sounds super fun, Mom. I will want to change into jeans and boots before we ride out. I'll toss what I need in the truck."

My daughter trotted out of the kitchen and was back a few moments later with her favorite cowboy style boots and a change of clothes. Lester and the kids left and only Mom and I remained in the kitchen.

"Did you get enough to eat, Mom?"

"Oh, my yes. Yvonne is picking me up shortly. I don't think I will want to eat the rest of the day."

A few hours later I picked Arista up and we drove out to Raccoon Hollow Trailhead. There were many trails to choose from and the scenery was always pretty. I unloaded the equine while Arista changed clothes in the truck, then she joined me beside the trailer.

"When was the last time we rode together Momma?"

I thought for a minute while I checked the girths on the saddles. "Gosh it's probably been six months ago."

Arista climbed atop Spot. The Appaloosa gelding was a birthday present from her Uncle Jacob. "See I thought so too. We should do it more often. It would be cool if Zoey and Brandy could ride with us too."

I swung into my saddle. "I know Zoey can ride but can Brandy?"

"I'm not sure, she's never said. Huh."

We rode in silence for a while and admired the countryside. The ample sunlight on my shoulders felt warm and cheery.

We were about an hour into our ride when Arista asked, "Momma, do you think you'll ever decide to date again?"

I hadn't been expecting that question. My muscles tensed and my breath caught. I couldn't prove it, but it seemed as though my mule noticed the change in my demeanor. He stopped abruptly and snorted. Arista, who was riding beside us, stopped her horse and turned to face me.

"Um, I don't know. Maybe. Why do you ask?"

"Ian and I were talking, and ya know, we are getting older. When we grow up and move out, you'll be all alone. Except for Grams but she is already really old..."

Arista let her voice trail off. The expression on her face made it clear she didn't want to mention the eventual passing of her grandmother, but it was inferred.

Arista nudged her horse around and started up the trail. "We want you to be happy and not be lonely."

I sat in stunned silence atop BB for a moment. He pawed the ground. I took that to mean he didn't like being left behind by the other horse. *My daughter, fifteen going on thirty, just encouraged me to find a boyfriend so I'll have someone to 'hang' with when I'm old. What on Earth do I do with this?*

I was about seventy-five yards behind Arista, so I urged BB forward. The mule didn't need any encouragement. He hit his foxtrot gait, an astonishingly smooth gait that covered a lot of ground quickly, and we were caught up with them in no time.

"Arista, I can appreciate how you and Ian feel. I want y'all to be happy, too. I've considered the possibility of dating again. It's hard for me to take that step though. In my heart I'm married to your daddy. Michael isn't an easy man to forget." Tears welled in my eyes, and I blinked them back.

"Momma, no one wants you to forget about Daddy. Maybe live some new experiences."

We came to a fork in the trail, and we stopped. I pulled the map out of my saddle bag and handed it to Arista. It was good map reading practice for her plus it gave me time to think.

I stood in my stirrups and stretched. "I'll think it over. Sooner rather than later as it happens since Dr. Spencer invited me to go to dinner with him." I fidgeted with my reins and when I glanced up at my daughter, she was grinning at me.

Arista handed the map back to me. "That's awesome! I noticed him checking you out at the chili supper. You're gonna go, right?"

My face felt warm, and it had nothing to do with the sun. I shrugged. "I don't know. He has a nice laugh, and it might be fun."

"Plus, he's pretty cute for an old guy." Arista winked.

I blinked several times. "What? He's not old and neither am I for that matter."

She laughed. "I knew that would get you fired up."

"Smart aleck, which way do we go?"

Arista pointed down the trail to the left. "If we go that way, we will be back at the truck in ninety minutes or so. The other way is much longer."

I checked the time and considered the amount of daylight left. "Good call, let's go."

The trail back wound downhill and flattened out on the edge of a clearing. I knew from past experience in the spring and summer it filled with wildflowers. I made a mental note to bring Arista back then. *Maybe we could bring her friends. Hmm. It would be a nice place to picnic with a handsome vet too. Sans the kids.*

Surprise at the turn of my own thoughts caused my face to flush again. Rather than spend time thinking about that, I nudged my gaited mule into a running walk and lost myself in the present moment. It was like floating.

"Mom! Jeez what's the rush?" Arista's horse had to lope to catch us. "I love this horse, but he isn't as smooth as BB."

"Spot is supposed to be part Tennessee Walker. He has a couple gears you haven't found yet. Spend more time riding him, experiment with different speeds. I think he will surprise you."

We took advantage of the easier terrain. I showed her how to encourage her mount into a running walk. It took several tries, but once he got it, the smile on my daughter's face rivaled the sun.

"That's a good job. You'll want to practice that soon, while you and Spot remember how the gait feels. Horses are tactile learners. They remember more of what they feel and less of what you say."

Arista nodded. "Thanks Momma. This has been a good day."

"It has indeed." My eyes may have leaked a bit. Probably dust.

Around the next curve the trail narrowed and became steep again. We walked our mounts in companionable silence until we reached the truck.

After loading the equine, I closed and latched the trailer door. It was late afternoon and the warmth we enjoyed earlier diminished as the wind picked up. I was relieved to crawl into the cab of the pickup truck.

Arista ran her hands up and down her arms. "Gosh it got chilly fast. I hope the fireplace is going when we get home."

"Me too! I was thinking about grabbing some pizzas from ZaCel on the way home. How does that sound?" It had been a few weeks since we'd stopped into the Pizza Cellar, aka, ZaCel and I was having withdrawals.

"Omg, Mom, that sounds fantastic. Ian will be pi, um, sad he didn't get to come with us."

I laughed. "He will forgive us once he starts eating."

We walked into the Pizza Cellar and took a seat at the bar. The proprietor, Tony, greeted us. "Hello Fen, Arista, good to see ya! I'll be right there." He delivered a loaded pizza to the only other customers in the room. Two couples sat in a booth in the back corner with a pitcher of beer. They exclaimed how wonderful the pizza looked when Tony placed it in front of them. His pizzas were the best in the region.

Tony came over and wiped the bar down in front of us. It was more out of habit than necessity. "What can I get started for you ladies? Where's Ian?"

"Ian's at home. He went to school today. I went

riding with Mom," Arista said.

"Oh yeah, I heard a rumor you were suspended. I heard you beat up a boy twice your size for gettin' fresh. Way to go girl!" Tony's smile spread ear to ear.

I shook my head. "While it was justified, please don't encourage her." I used my most official mom voice. "I know news travels fast, but how in the world did you hear about it?"

"Oh well, Rebecca came in. You know how she is." Tony shrugged.

I nodded. "How about two large pizzas, stuffed and loaded but no olives."

"You got it, Fen. You want a coffee for you and a Vanilla Cola shot for Arista?"

"Sure, thanks, Tony."

Thirty minutes or so later, we were back in the truck and headed home with two scrumptious-smelling pizzas in the back seat. Tony had included, at no charge, a new dessert pizza. He explained it's a new recipe and he gives one to his best customers because he wants honest feedback.

"Momma, do you think people will think I'm a bully when they hear what happened?"

I thought for a moment and glanced at my daughter. I was proud of her for standing up for her friend. She had a big heart and anyone that knew her well knew she was miles away from being a bully. "Honey, I suppose it depends on the version they hear and what they want to believe. People who know you or know our family won't think you're a bully. Others will make up their minds once they've met you. There'll always be a few who believe everything they hear and don't have the good sense to do their own research. To heck with them, they're a waste of time anyway. Does that help?"

"Yep, I get it. Thanks, Momma. I love you."

"I love you too, kid."

We pulled into the driveway a few moments later. I parked the truck and trailer near the gate leading to the horse barn so unloading would be a snap. It didn't take long to unload the equine. I decided to leave the trailer hooked up for the night. The food was still warm when we sat down to eat. Arista filled Ian, Lester, and her grandma in on our day and inquired about theirs.

I was a little nervous that she would spill the beans about Dr. Spencer asking me out. I wasn't ready for it to become common knowledge yet. Arista didn't mention it to the group, but I suspected she would tell her twin later. There wasn't much they didn't share.

An hour or so after the rest of my family turned in for the night, Sophia pitched a frantic barking fit at the back door. The last time she did it involved a skunk, several baths, and one week of quarantine in the laundry room. "Nope, little girl, if you have to potty, I will take you on a leash, but there will be no running amok at this time of night."

Unfazed by the leash, Sophia dove out the door and pulled with all her ten pounds of furious self. Her little legs scrambled for traction. I swear she tossed me the stink eye for not moving as fast as she wanted.

I held the door open a moment too long, and a tiny yellow and white streak shot out past me and the dog. "Fabulous! Come back here you little runt." The kitten tore across the driveway, under the paddock fence and into the stall area where BB was munching hay. I heard BB nicker softly. The mule liked cats almost as much as I did, so I wasn't worried about the kitten's safety.

I refused to give in to the small dog's demands. Every time she yanked on my arm, we slowed down. I would retrieve the wayward kitty in a moment. I shined my flashlight around and hoped to avoid any skunk encounters. When the beam of light hit the horse trailer, I noticed the hay compartment door open. "Hmm, that's strange." I walked over and closed the door after a quick inspection of the latch. Sophia was overly curious about the area around the trailer door. Her nose on high alert, at least she'd stopped pulling on her leash. "Come on pup, do your business and let's catch that goofy cat and go to bed." Sophia looked up at me and cocked her head. I took it as a question but didn't know the answer.

I opened the barn door and flicked on the light, eternal gratitude to my dad for having installed lights in the barn. Sophia ran to the end of her leash and growled. She stood stiff legged with her nose pointed at the stacked hay bales. I blinked several times to make sense of what I saw. There were two boots in the aisle. They moved.

CHAPTER 21

I gripped my Maglite like a club. "You there, whoever the hell you are, don't move. I'm armed." My voice sounded much steadier than I felt. *I should call someone. Who? I don't want the kids or Lester out here. Jacob is out. Crap, my phone is on the kitchen counter.* "Who are you and why are you in my barn?"

"Por favor no dispares. No te haré daño. No tenía adónde ir," said the unknown person.

My Spanish language skills were passable, but no need for them to know that. "Great, now give that to me in English," I said.

"Please lady, do not shoot me. I am hurt and I have nowhere to go."

The male voice, a deep baritone sounded scared. "Do you have any weapons? If you do, toss them out gently, into the middle of the barn."

"No, I am not armed. No gun no knife," he said.

"Put your hands up and step out here where I can see you. Move slow."

The man stepped from behind the hay into the light.

He took a few steps toward me with his hands in the air. I noticed his right shirt sleeve was covered in blood and he wore no coat.

"That's far enough," I said.

BB stuck his head over the wall of the stall and nickered. The man reached over and stroked the mule's nose. I recognized him as the larger Hispanic man from the park. When I saw him then he hadn't been bloody, his friend was still alive and so was Darrin McNamara. Sophia, the little traitor, ran over and flopped on her back. This is her go-to move when meeting strangers. She would wiggle until they relented and rubbed her belly. Fine watch dog she is.

The man who stood before me was very large. Six feet, four inches at least and broad. Linebacker for a good team. His dark brown eyes were kind and intelligent. I detected not an ounce of menace from him. *Still, better safe than sorry.* "So, what's your story? Why are you here?"

The big man wobbled. In a blink he was on the ground. He sat there with a stunned expression on his face. "Perdóneme. Me mareé. Uh, dizzy is the English word I think."

I watched him shake his head. "When was the last time you ate something or had water?" I asked. I assessed the likely causes. Dehydration was at the top of my list, followed by low blood sugar. I wasn't discounting the blood loss and possibility of infection. I'd gotten a good look at his right hand. There were stubs where two of his fingers should have been. I considered the grisly discovery of amputated fingers the other day. Wasn't hard to do the math.

"I was eating from the dumpster behind the pizza

restauranté. I drank from your mule tank when I got here," he explained.

Dammit. "Stay put. I'll be right back with some food. Give me any trouble and I will drop you right here and feed you to my pigs." I stalked out of the barn. Sophia stayed with the strange man. Traitorous pooch.

"Si, senorá, no trouble here."

I loaded up my cooler on wheels with some water, a half dozen sandwiches, chips, cookies and a thermos of coffee. Technically the coffee was for me, I intended to sit down and extract the whole story from my barn guest. I wouldn't invite this stranger, who may be Mexican mafia but I doubted it, into my home. I also wasn't going to allow him to starve or freeze. I grabbed some old blankets we use for animal emergencies or camping. They're clean and serviceable. My first aid supplies were depleted over the last month or so. I grabbed what I had and trudged back to the barn.

I continue to be stunned by the animals that live with me. When I walked into the barn, there was the large guy seated on the ground. Sophia curled up on his lap and the kitten sat in the man's hand, snuggled against his neck.

The guy looked up at me and smiled. "El gato y el perro son muy simpáticos."

I smiled back. "They like you. I will trust their judgement for now. How about you eat and tell me your story. Start with your name. My name is Fen."

"Holá Fen. I am Carlos."

Carlos ate two sandwiches and half a bag of chips while he told me how he came to be in Blossom Bluff,

Missouri. He stopped eating when he got to the part about his fingers being removed. His eyes watered and his voice cracked. "So now I'm trying to figure out how to get home without getting killed or worse, deported."

I sipped my coffee. The story captivated me until the finger part. I'd listened without interruption while Carlos filled me in on the last couple weeks of his life. I'd made some decisions based on what I'd heard but also the *vibe* of the tale.

"Here's the deal, Carlos. I believe you and am willing to help you provided I can also keep my family safe. You were a victim of a terrible crime, and you witnessed an even worse crime. You must tell the police. Our sheriff is a good man. He won't break the law for you, but he will protect you. I believe there is a law that keeps people from being deported if they have witnessed a major crime. I will have to research it to make sure I'm remembering it right. No guarantees on not getting deported, but I feel certain we can keep you safe if you cooperate."

Carlos raised his eyes to meet mine. After a moment he nodded.

"Okay, lets clean that wound up and have a look at it. I brought some supplies and also some blankets."

The wounds on Carlos' hand were difficult to look at, and I was relieved to see no indication of gangrene. He definitely needed more medical attention than what I could provide. For tonight this would have to do. We couldn't risk taking him to the hospital until the sheriff was on board.

Once his hand was cleaned and bandaged, Carlos grew sleepy. Pain, hunger and exposure to the weather can wear a body out. We positioned several square hay bales together to form a mattress and covered them with a tarp so it wouldn't be so scratchy. Carlos told me he didn't mind and had slept in worse places. Once he laid down and I heaped the blankets, he began to snore. Sophia whined when I tried to take her to the house, so I let her stay. She disappeared under the blankets with her new friend. I scooped the tiny kitten up and took him inside. He was too young to be outside on his own. He didn't complain.

I was eager to clean up and get to sleep. Reflection revealed a mostly good, if not strange, day. A check of the time told me it was almost midnight. *No wonder I'm tired.*

I fell fast asleep soon after my head hit the pillow. My dreams were an odd mish-mash of riding horses through fields filled with flowers, a river of blood running across a city street, and dancing fingers.

CHAPTER 22

I awoke Friday morning around six a.m. and felt tired and unsettled.

I showered and started breakfast. It was too early for polite people to call other polite people, but a text was less intrusive, and the situation demanded some urgency.

"Oh, kitty, politeness is underrated, but here it goes." I hit the send button. Within a few minutes, both Jana and Sheriff Peters responded.

"On my way."

I'd called an urgent breakfast meeting. I had a long story to tell and might as well get it over with.

I'd finished cooking breakfast and placed several chafing dishes in the warm oven while I waited for people to descend on the kitchen. A short while later, two sheriff's department SUVs pulled into the driveway. My brother Jacob followed behind them in his sports car. Ian and Arista hit the kitchen simultaneously. As everyone dug into breakfast, I explained the reason for the impromptu meeting. When

I got to the part about Carlos being in the barn, Jana and Uncle John put their forks down and started to get up.

"Please wait, there's more." I gestured with my hands to stop and sit. "Carlos will tell you his story. I have heard it, and I believe him. He needs help and protection."

"Fenreya, you are harboring a potential murderer and a probable illegal alien. If you weren't my oldest friend's daughter, I would have already arrested you."

"Uncle John, I understand you are upset with me. Please hear him out. He didn't kill or harm anyone. I'd bet on it. He's terrified and hurt." I wiped an errant tear off my cheek. I hadn't meant to get emotional.

I surveyed the faces around the table. The kids and Jacob were gaping at me as if I'd grown a second head. Jana was studying the food on her plate. I took it as an uncharacteristic sign of neutrality. Uncle John's face wore a mix of disappointment and concern.

After the meal, I asked Jacob to drive Ian to school since he'd missed the bus again. Arista wanted to follow Jana, the sheriff and me to the barn but I forbade it. I led them to the barn, and we found Carlos sitting on a hay bale eating the last of the sandwiches. I handed him a plate of breakfast food.

He took it with his good hand. "Gracias, Senora."

"Good morning, Carlos, I've brought Sheriff John Peters and his deputy, Jana, to talk with you. Please tell them everything you told me last night."

We sat across from Carlos to listen. He inhaled the eggs, wiped his mouth on his sleeve then set the plate aside.

"About three weeks ago I was outside the Home Depot in Tulsa with a few other men. We hoped for work that would be legal, and there hadn't been much of it for weeks. A little Mexican guy came up to me and offered me fifty dollars a day to travel with him and be his bodyguard. I told him I don't do that work but he promised I wouldn't have to do anything but stand around and look mean. He said my size would speak for me. His name was Eddie G. I went with him. We drove to Oklahoma City and picked up some boxes. He wouldn't tell me what was in them. Then we went south and east and stopped at many towns along the way. It was easy work at first. He paid me ahead of time so I could send money to my mother. We got to this big town in Arkansas and Eddie drove to the alley behind a food store. Some guys were waiting for us. They didn't have the money for the package Eddie brought them and they tried to take the package. We fought them off. Eddie pulled a knife and stuck one of them. We drove off and the package tore open. A bunch of pills spilled out and Eddie was real mad.

"We drove for hours and when we stopped for gas, I told him that I didn't like this work, and I was out. He said no and that he would turn me into ICE so I would get sent back. He said I would get the blame for sticking the man in Little Rock. Eddie said since he paid me early, I owed him money. Then last week we got to this town. We met with Darren, the man who died. He didn't have the money for his box of pills either, but he traded some other drugs to Eddie and promised to pay the rest on Saturday. When Saturday morning came, he and Eddie argued about the money. Darren said that the pills were short and the meth he'd given Eddie more than paid for it. He claimed we owed him money. Eddie didn't agree and made me hit the man. Then Darren left the park. We sat in Eddie's car, and a truck pulled up. Two guys got out and jumped us."

Carlos paused and took a drink of water. His face lost some color.

Sheriff Peters leaned forward. "What did the two guys look like, and do you know their names or the license plate number from their truck?"

"No sir, I know it was a dark truck. The guys were white. One was big like me but not as tall. The other one was smaller. His eyes showed no soul. He was the boss of the big man. They were mad. The big one pointed his gun at us, and the small one did the talking. He said he knew we were cartel and we were in their territory. Eddie used to like it when people thought he was with a cartel. It made him feel big and important. He tried to tell them that he was just a small-time steroid dealer, and he didn't know no cartel people. The white guys didn't believe him. They shot him and dumped him in the trash. The little one pulled out a big knife and told me to go home and tell all my cartel buddies to stay out of Dixie. He cut my fingers off. I must have passed out for a short time because they were gone. I was bleeding. Eddie was dead. I knew I had to get gone before they came back and decided to kill me too. I decided to hide until dark, so I drove down the tiny road over by the pizza store. Eddie's car was almost out of gas, and he kept all the money on him. I was stuck. I was eating out of the pizza place's trash for days. I saw the guys that hurt me and shot Eddie go into the building. I was scared they would see me or find me. I crawled into her horse trailer because I figured anywhere would be better than staying there."

Jana had been taking notes the entire time Carlos spoke. She tapped her pen on her notebook. "Did the men ever call each other by name? Did you notice any scars, tattoos or anything like that about either of them?"

Carlos scrunched his face as he thought. "The big one called the other one Bamma. I think they both had some tats, but I don't know what they were. I was too freaked out to notice."

I noticed Uncle John's expression change. He paled. *He's never shown an ounce of fear in all the years. Oh goodness, what could this be about?* Jana must have noticed, too.

She asked, "What is it, Sheriff?"

He stood up and put his hands in his pockets. "Carlos, I'm willing to believe your story, and provided it checks out, are you willing to testify in court? Doing so can keep you in the country, but you will be in danger. These people are very bad people. You might be safer back in Mexico."

Carlos shook his head. "No sir, I am not safer in Mexico. I ran from there after I saw some real cartel people do some very bad things. More bad even than these two white guys. My whole family left and came to the States. I can't go back." His hands were shaking and his voice trembled.

Uncle John nodded. His jaw set, an air of decision emanated from him. "Okay son, here's what's gonna happen. You will stay hidden for now. I will contact the Department of Immigration and Naturalization and start the process to get a temporary, emergency green card since you're a material witness to a murder. I will arrange for some discreet medical attention and find you a place to stay that isn't a barn. You will keep your word and testify, you will stay completely out of trouble and off the streets until we get this figured out. Are we clear?"

"Si, yes, sir." Carlos heaved a deep breath.

His face lit with obvious relief.

I let out the breath I'd been holding. "He can stay here for a while, until other arrangements can be made. Not in the barn, there is a small apartment above the shop."

The sheriff assured us he would file the form for *S Immigrant* status. It's a special type of green card for persons acting as a witness or informant for law enforcement. He explained he could file that form but the other type of exemption for victims of crime would need to be filled out by Carlos or his legal representative. Uncle John thought Carlos would qualify for this program, but it was outside his area of experience.

Jana snapped some photos of Carlos, his injured hand and took his fingerprints using a digital gizmo I'd never seen before.

"Fen, please tell Jacob I'll be back later." She looked pointedly at Carlos.

I surmised she wanted him to know she would be back as a passive warning to behave. I hid my smile. Jana was a fiercely protective friend. I wouldn't want to be on her bad side.

"Señora Fen, I am fine in the barn. You do not have to open your home to me."

"Nonsense, it's no trouble. Help me gather up these dishes and take them to the house. We'll get you settled. You can clean up while I run to town and grab some more bandages."

The shop building sat about 50 yards from the house. It was a sturdy building with a concrete floor, where the tools lived. Ian and Lester were spending a fair amount of time out there working on their antique tractor project. I showed Carlos to the apartment. It was a tiny studio type of set up. I never understood why Daddy equipped the shop with its own apartment, but today I was glad he had. Even though I believed Carlos to be innocent of the recent crimes, he had been an accessory to drug trafficking. I would instruct Arista to keep the house doors locked just in case.

Jacob arrived home as I was about to leave. I delivered Jana's message and brought him up to speed on everything else. He took it in stride. Another thing I loved about my brother.

I grabbed a parking spot right in front of the drug store on the square. The plan to restock my first aid supplies completed in no time. The aroma of fresh brewed coffee, pastries laced with vanilla and cinnamon wafted out of Cones and Scones. I was hooked. In I went.

Agatha greeted me with her usual vigor.

"Hey, Fen, what'll it be?"

"Good morning, Agatha. I'd like my normal cappuccino with an extra shot, a cheese Danish, and a box of goodies to go. Surprise me."

"Sure thing, coming right up."

I settled into one of the chairs near the kitchen entrance and focused on my phone.

"Hi, Fen, mind if I sit down?"

I felt my cheeks heat when my gaze met Dr. Will Spencer's eyes. "Sure."

"Is that, 'sure you mind' or 'sure sit down'?" His eyes sparkled; an eyebrow raised.

Omg, what is it about this guy that causes me to sound ridiculous? "Um. Yeah, you can sit." I gestured at the opposite chair. Dr. Spencer sat down and peered at me.

"Would you join me for dinner this evening?"

"Um sure. I mean yes, that sounds nice." I regretted my current messy hair, no makeup status.

We arranged to meet for an early supper at his apartment and then go to a movie. Will assured me he wasn't cheap, he loved to cook for more than one person.

Agatha brought my order to the table and winked at me which made my cheeks heat again. I said goodbye to Will and escaped the coffee shop to the quiet safety of my truck. *Good grief, I haven't blushed this much since 7th grade. I've got to get a handle on it.*

When I stopped at the convenience store to fill the gas tank, I saw a small blue car and a dark green truck parked cop style. The driver of the blue car was the man I'd seen leaving the vet's office. I couldn't see the driver of the truck. The windows were tinted, and it was facing away from me. Carlos said the guys were in a dark truck. *Girl, the world is full of dark trucks. Don't borrow trouble.*

I drove home and checked in with Mom and Arista, then I headed over to see Carlos and change the bandages on his hand. Jacob popped in and introduced himself to Carlos.

I needed to settle my nerves before my date. The weather was still unseasonably nice for mid-December so I saddled BB and went for a ride. A couple hours of saddle therapy does wonders for the mind. Everything else needed to be showered, exfoliated, and dressed in something other than ratty, faded jeans. I'd formed a plan for the evening, knew what to wear and made a mental list of conversation topics. I also had a nagging feeling that I'd missed something important.

Will was expecting me to arrive at 5:15 p.m. I ran five minutes late, but I looked good in a cream blouse, an emerald-green suede skirt and a tartan shawl. I'd opted for low-heeled black, dressy boots since we'd planned to walk the three blocks to the old movie theater to see a vintage movie. The entrance to Will's loft apartment was accessed by stairs behind the building. The same parking lot one Darren McNamara died in a few days before. A shiver ran down my spine at the memory of his body impaled on the hay spike. I hurried up the stairs and knocked on the door. A faint "Be right there," emanated from inside the apartment.

I gazed out in the direction of the street. The small blue car drove up the street. *It could be a different car, right?* Behind me the door opened, and Will stepped out to greet me. He had a kitchen towel slung over his shoulder and his hair was messy. "Hi, Fen, come on in. Gosh you look great." He tossed the towel on the counter and ran a hand through his hair. I suppressed a giggle.

Will turned out to be a good cook. He fixed chicken cordon bleu, roasted sweet potatoes, and steamed broccoli. Halfway through the meal, I finally felt relaxed.

"I'd wanted to make cheesecake for dessert but I ran out of time so I thought we could stop after the movie for something sweet. If you want to."

"I'm already full, it was a lovely meal. Thank you for cooking. Do you know which movie is scheduled for tonight?"

"The title is *Meet Me in St. Louis*. It's a musical set in 1904. It's considered a Christmas classic because Judy Garland sings *Have Yourself a Merry Little Christmas*. If it sounds lame, we can drive to the bigger theater in Branson."

"I've never seen it, but my mom loves that film. Besides why drive an hour to a packed town when we can walk a couple blocks and enjoy the holiday lights?"

Will smiled. "Excellent."

He wouldn't let me help clear the table, so I spent a few moments looking around his living room. The apartment was more spacious than I'd imagined. There were several framed photos on the wall above the couch. One photo was of Will and a smaller man. They stood beside a shiny dark green truck.

"Who is in this picture with you?" My brain was trying to connect some dots.

He stepped beside me, the towel back on his shoulder. Will pointed at the photo in question. "That is my cousin Bobby. He'd just gotten the truck and was so proud of it."

"Does he live nearby?" *Could Bobby be Bamma? A big guy and a little guy in a dark truck. But no, that made zero sense. Will was running with his dog the day Eddie G. was killed.*

"No, he got married and moved to Oregon. Why?"

"No reason really, he looked familiar is all." It was a

lie, and I regretted it. Brutus, Will's dog bumped my leg. Dogs know many things.

"Brutus, stop that. Don't slobber on her pretty dress. I'm sorry Fen." He handed me the towel.

I laughed and patted the dog's huge head. "No problem, he was so well-behaved during dinner I forgot he was here. Are we ready to go?"

When we got to the lower landing outside Will's apartment, he patted his pockets. "Oh shoot, I left my wallet upstairs. I'm sorry, I'll be right back." I watched him hurry up the steps. If I hadn't been distracted by the nice view, I might have heard the man come up behind me.

CHAPTER 23

A meaty hand closed over my mouth and a hoarse voice whispered in my ear. "Not a sound bitch. You just had to be nosy. Always watching me."

My mind raced to make the connections. All I knew was that this was a big guy, and if I let him drag me from this area, my chances of survival dropped exponentially. I shifted my weight and tried to elbow my attacker in his gut, but he held me too tightly. Barking erupted from Will's apartment. Brutus knew. Would he be helpful? A dog that flunked K9 academy for being too nice.

The apartment door opened. Brutus was fighting to get out. Unaware of my situation, Will tried to push him back inside.

"Brutus, what is wrong with you? Get inside, you aren't allowed in the theater." Will glanced over his should toward me and his face paled. "Hey, get your hands off her!"

My attacker raised his other arm. The gun he held pointed at Will. "Don't be stupid, Doc."

Brutus rushed past Will and bounded down the stairs. Several shots rang out and pinged off the iron stairs. Brutus yelped and raced toward us. I shoved the gun arm as hard as I could. I completed the twist when the big arm around me loosened and I jammed my attacker in the eye with my thumb. Brutus bit into the guy's leg and he screamed in pain. The man tried to level the gun at the dog, but a throat punch distracted him. The gun fell from his grasp when he grabbed for his throat. I kicked the man squarely in the groin and when he doubled over, I slammed his face with my knee. He toppled backwards. Brutus continued to clutch and tug at the man's right leg.

Will arrived and kicked the gun aside. He put his hands on my arms. I wheeled to face him, ready for another fight.

"Whoa now, easy slugger." He took a step back and held up his hands. "I'm one of the good guys. "Brutus, enough. Heel."

The attacker, who I now recognized as the man in the blue Toyota, writhed on the ground. Brutus limped over to Will and sat down. He whined. There were bloody paw prints on the concrete where the dog trod.

The vet sprang to action. "Oh no, Brut! Let me take a look. You're a good boy."

I stomped on our attacker's hand as he tried to crawl away. "You shot a dog, you worthless piece of trash."

Sirens sounded in the distance. Someone heard the shots and called it in. Several minutes later the lot filled with flashing lights for the second time in a week.

Officer Mike, of our city police department was the first one on scene. He took custody of my attacker, whose name turned out to be Donald Aron Gibson.

Mr. Gibson complained loud and long about his injuries and threatened to sue me, the dog and the whole town.

Mike laughed at him. "Yeah buddy, you think you got it bad? You should be grateful it was her and a dog that got you instead of her mule."

I gaped at the officer. "You heard about that?"

"Heck yeah, it's a small town." He stuffed the cuffed Gibson into the rear of his patrol car.

Sheriff Peters was second on the scene. He'd arrived in a cloud of gravel. "I had a feeling this call involved something to do with you, Fen. Are you hurt?"

"No sir, I'm okay. That creep fired several shots and missed everyone except Will's dog." I pointed to where Will knelt on the ground next to Brutus.

Sheriff Peters snapped a couple photos, with his phone, of the gun on the ground before he collected it in a plastic evidence bag. "Doctor Spencer, I'm sorry about your dog. Is he going to be all right?"

Will stood. "I want to get him to the clinic and take some X-rays. I think he will be fine. He was lucky. The bullet grazed his front leg. The blood has already stopped.

Brutus limped over to me and wagged his tail. I bent down and hugged him. "You are my hero, such a good boy. So very brave." Brutus grinned and panted.

Jana and Jacob rolled up in his car. Jana was not dressed as a deputy but was in "cop mode" anyhow. I assured them I was fine.

"Captain, since you're here would you mind taking Fen's statement and canvas the scene for shell casings? I'm going to accompany Dr. Spencer to his clinic with Brutus. I want to document the gunshot wound with photos."

"Sure thing, Sheriff." Jana looked at Jacob and shrugged. "You didn't want to see that movie anyway."

"That's not what I meant. It seems like if you want to watch moldy old movies, we can do that at home." My brother shook his head.

Will and I exchanged a look. "Moldy old movie? Were you guys going to see 'Meet Me in St. Louis' tonight?" When they both nodded, Will and I laughed.

"That's where we were going before that jackass ruined our first date and shot my dog."

Jacob stuck his hands in his pockets. "Dude, that sucks. Maybe we can double up. Maybe even catch a movie from this century."

Will promised to call me later, after he'd done a thorough examination of Brutus. He and Uncle John headed for the vet clinic in their respective vehicles. I gave my statement to Jana and pointed out the places where Gibson attacked me, as well as the direction of the shots he'd fired. She recovered several shell casings and found a bullet lodged in a wooden door frame. That bullet had some blood and a couple of hairs stuck to it. I watched Jana extract, collect, and label the evidence. Gibson would be going away. I'd yet to figure out why the crazy bastard attacked me.

Jacob left his car for Jana and rode home with me. I'd watched the silent agreement between them that I should not be left alone.

Once we arrived at the house, I asked Jake to fetch Carlos from the studio. I only wanted to tell the eventful tale once more before I collapsed into bed. The kids peppered me with questions about my date the moment I walked in. One look at my disheveled appearance changed their excitement to worried anger.

"I'm fine. Give me a moment to make some coffee and change my clothes. I will tell you everything."

I washed my face and donned comfy sweats. The kitchen was fuller than expected and abuzz with chatter when I entered.

Carlos arrived. He appeared overwhelmed by my children's questions.

Jacob was on his phone. "Lester, how'd you hear about it?"

He placed a cup of coffee in front of me.

"I heard about the ruckus on my police scanner. Ian texted to tell me you were involved."

I eyed the coffee with suspicion. "Is there special sauce in that?"

The old man winked at me. "Drink it and find out."

I took that challenge. The liquid burned all the way down my throat. I took a deep breath and launched the story of events. Once I was done, questions hammered me. The main one being "who is this Gibson guy and why did he attack you?" *Wouldn't I like to know.*

"That is the million-dollar question," I said.

Jacob held his phone out to everyone in the room. "Jana sent me this picture. Do any of you know anything about this guy? Especially you, Carlos."

Ian and Arista gasped.

"Mom, that's our janitor up at school." Arista followed up with, "That guy always gave me the wiggins. He's got a creepy vibe."

"I've seen him hanging around the jocks. There's a rumor that he passes out steroids," Ian added.

Carlos studied the picture. "I saw that guy. Eddie delivered a small box of pills to him last week. The guy paid Eddie and didn't cause no trouble so I didn't really notice him."

Jana arrived about thirty minutes later in Jake's car. She looked tired and grateful to accept the coffee, sans the special sauce, and pie. She expressed interest in what Carlos and the kids had to say about Gibson.

She wiped pie crumbs from the table and dusted them onto her empty plate. "The suspect refused to talk to anyone. No priors but his prints seem to match the prints found on the bat that killed McNamara. The gun we recovered from the scene tonight is the same caliber as the weapon that killed Eddie G. Carlos are you sure he wasn't with the guys that attacked you and Eddie?"

"Si, Miss Officer. I'm sure he wasn't there when Eddie was shot and they hurt me." Carlos winced.

I knew from the expression on his face the memory of that day would stab his psyche for years to come.

I refilled the coffee mugs, and we all migrated into the office to stare at the *Murder Board.* Carlos broke the silence. "So, I am *Missing Finger's Guy?"*

Arista blushed. "Sorry Carlos, we didn't know who you were and none of us have taken time to update the board with all the new information." She marked through Missing Finger Guy and wrote *Carlos* instead.

"We might as well change *Dumpster Guy* to *Eddie G* now that we know his name. We need to add Donald Gibson as a suspect," I said.

"Those two guys in the dark truck, are they up there yet?" Carlos asked, his voice so quiet.

Fear and uncertainty rolled off him like rain from a stopped-up gutter. I took a moment to imagine his situation.

After a few moments of studying the updated

information, we all silently agreed it was time to call it a day. Lester bade everyone goodnight and headed for his truck. I missed him living with us in the house but knew he was happy to be back in his own place. Carlos trudged back to the studio apartment. The rest of us headed off to our respective rooms.

I wedged myself into bed between two cats and a dog. "How can such small creatures take up so much space?"

CHAPTER 24

The Saturday morning sunlight was brilliant and cheerful. It streamed in my bedroom window and warmed the belly of the rotund calico. "My stars, it must be late for it to be that bright." Issy yawned and stretched. I checked my inner calendar. There was nowhere I was obligated to be today. *A rare and wonderful feeling, think I'll stay in bed.*

A small yellow and white puff ball sailed through the sunbeam. The little dude batted at nothing or perhaps dust motes. He landed on Issy, she yowled and he rolled away, popped up and kept running. I laughed. *So much for sleeping in.* I threw the covers off and got out of bed. Issy was not amused.

My kitchen bustled with people. I grabbed some coffee and took a seat on the end of the island. "Hey, Momma."

"G'morning, Mom."

More words tumbled toward me.

"We want to go roller skating with a bunch of kids from school. It's at the rink over in Branson. Uncle Jake said he'd take us. Can we go? Pleeeaaasse?"

My children drew the word out as if the longer it was, the more apt I'd be to let them go. "Y'all can go provided the list of chores I gave you three days ago is properly done."

They scurried off to find and check the list.

Jacob refilled his coffee and started another pot. "You remember when we used to go skating over in Branson? That was a sure way to raise your *cool score.*"

"I do remember. It was so much fun. It's surprising roller rinks survived the video game revolution. Seems most folks, kids included, would rather sit on their butts and play video games. I'm grateful my kids like a variety of activities."

"I'm proud of my niece and nephew, you've done a helluva fine job raising them, sissy."

"Thanks, baby bro."

An hour later I had the house to myself. The quiet unnerved me a little. I should spend the day in my jewelry studio but there would be other days for that. The weather was too gorgeous to pass up a day of riding.

When I got to the barn I found Carlos cleaning the tack and beating the dust and hair out of the saddle blankets. I was astonished. "Hey Carlos, whatcha doing?"

The big man jumped. "Good morning, Miss Fen. Your hospitality makes me want to help out. I can do many things but thought I would start here in the barn."

"Thanks, I appreciate your efforts. I've noticed you like animals and they like you."

"Si, I love them all, big and little. My favorite job back home before we were forced to leave was, I worked at the zoo near Guadalajara. I felt sad that they were locked up, but the care was good and I made friends there."

"I'm going for a ride around the property and close country roads. If you ride and want to join me, the big grey horse is gentle but hasn't been out in a while."

Carlos' face lit up at the invitation. "Si, señora, me encanta montar a caballo!"

"Carlos, you slip into Spanish when you get excited about something. I think you said you love to ride horses?"

"Yes, exacta mentee. Um. Exactly what I said."

We rode down the lane and out unto the road. I was curious how Tammy and Brandy were doing since they moved back home. *They live close enough to ride by and take a peek.* I wondered if they'd gotten the ransacked house set to rights, but I was reluctant to pop by there. *They don't know about Carlos yet and the fewer people who know about him the better for now.*

We walked the equine down past Lester's driveway, up the hill and turned around at Brandy's Road. "I think we should check the fence along the road, ride down by the creek on the far side of our place and then head back. By then it'll be time for a snack."

Carlos agreed with me in two languages.

We rode past our lane and continued east down the road. Inspection of the fence revealed a few minor issues. "Those tiny things need to be fixed before they become big things."

"Si, Miss Fen, the big things are what lets animals get out and run off."

Carlos told me stories about his time working for the zoo. A storm knocked over some trees, they smashed down a fence and they were all conscripted to rounding up several small herds of assorted creatures. Most were from the petting zoo area and thankfully none of the apex predators had escaped.

We got to the old logging road that ran down the east edge of our property. Daddy secured it years ago with a large iron gate. We rarely used it for access and kept it locked out of habit. The key was in a waterproof container under a rock. I dismounted and did the open, close and relock routine.

During the ride, a few vehicles drove past at a respectable speed, and we hadn't paid them any attention. I'd clicked the padlock shut and went to remount my mule when an engine roared around the curve and braked so hard the tires squealed and smoked. The dark green truck was vaguely familiar to me. It slid to a stop within a couple inches of the iron gate.

Both equine spooked. Carlos stayed on his and he began to point and shout. In Spanish. In the chaos it took me a minute to figure out two very important things. 1. Carlos recognized the men in the truck and was terrified of them. 2. They were getting out of the truck and *Holy crap on a cracker is that a gun?*

I clung to my saddle while BB pulled himself together. He paused his flight long enough for me to get in the saddle. Carlos and the big grey horse were well in front and headed south on the overgrown path. I needed to catch up since he didn't know the best way.

BB pulled in front of the grey horse, and I yelled for Carlos to follow me. Several shots rang out. Carlos shouted something I couldn't understand. I was well and truly tired of being shot at, this was the second time in two days.

I couldn't remember the Braucherei chant against firearms, so I conjured a footman instead. *If I live through this Auntie is going to kick my bum for forgetting my training. That was the whole purpose of memorizing the chants after all.*

Footman, Footman I conjure thee
Get us where we need to be
Afterward I set thee free

We rode down the old trail and cut through the woods to our southernmost pasture. My brain caught up and decided that we'd outrun the guys for now. Even if they could get the gate open, their truck wouldn't make it very far down the narrow trail. I pulled BB to a stop. The grey horse stopped beside us. Carlos was pale and breathing heavy. Blood ran down the side of the horse, but it wasn't the horse's blood.

"Oh, my Goddess, Carlos! You're hit. Shit. Where are you hit?"

He pointed to his right side. I dug in my saddle bag for the first aid kit. I packed all the gauze in there, which wasn't enough on the wound. The tape wouldn't stick, and I didn't have any way to tie the makeshift bandage in place.

"Carlos, you need to keep pressure on this. We need to get to the house, then the hospital. You gotta stay awake buddy and don't fall off. You understand?"

"Si, don't fall off."

I watched his eyes roll back, refocus and he wobbled. The grey horse began to fidget. Horses are prey animals and don't appreciate the smell of blood. Daddy used to take this particular grey horse elk hunting and BB was the smartest, calmest mule ever. I could only expect them to put up with so much, it was time to get moving again. I clipped a lead line on the grey horse and headed for the house.

I knew I would need backup soon. I fished my phone out of my pocket. No bars. *Well of course, that would have been too freaking simple.*

The gate between the south field and the middle field wasn't locked so it was easy to open. I didn't even dismount. Closing it while managing the grey horse and checking on Carlos was trickier. Being out in the middle of an open field was nerve wracking after being shot at. I reasoned there was almost no way those guys could figure out where we went, nor could they catch us on foot. I opted to hug the tree line on the west side of the field. We were about a hundred yards from the house and two bars popped up on my phone. *Two whole bars, Blessed Be!*

I called Uncle John, it went to voice mail. *Dammit!* I called Jana and she picked up. She was over on the far side of the county working a minor accident. "I'll call the sheriff and send an ambulance your way. Be safe, girl. I'm on my way. These nice folks are going to have to exchange insurance info and get over it." I thanked her and we clicked off the call.

I shoved my phone in my pocket and picked up the pace. We were almost there.

CHAPTER 25

The daylight faded faster than I'd hoped due to a large bank of clouds. The barn was in sight. We approached it from the east. The house sat to the east of the barn. BB stopped and stood stock still. His ears pointed forward. "Come on BB, almost there. We have to save Carlos." The mule wouldn't budge. "Seriously? You pick now? You never do this....oh." He stamped his foot. I took the hint. I dismounted and crept up to the rear of the barn. I peeked around the side. *Well hell.*

A dark green truck was parked in the middle of the driveway. It blocked my truck from leaving even if we could get to it. I saw two people in the front seat. Their windows were down. It's a wonder they hadn't heard us ride up, we hadn't been stealthy.

Arista's horse was out in the paddock. He noticed us and being the good, friendly boy that he is, he nickered and trotted in our direction. *Dammit, can I catch a break please.*

My heart hammered and my hands began to sweat. A bunch of things happened at once.

The smaller guy got out of the truck and leaned against it. He held a large knife, endeared to hill folk everywhere as "an Arkansas toothpick." He began to clean his fingernails with the point.

"Hey, Milo, they're back."

The bigger guy, presumed to be *Milo,* got out of the truck and dragged a third person out of the rear seat.

There was a loud thump behind me. I spun around and saw poor Carlos had fallen from his horse. He lay on the ground and moaned. I remembered the chant against guns and hoped it worked on knives too.

The grey horse trotted off when his rider hit the ground. Poor beast had all he was going to take for today. I slunk over to Carlos and whispered to keep quiet, "I'll be back for you as soon as possible. Those guys are here and I'm going to deal with them. Help is coming. I got a call out to Jana."

The only response from Carlos was a weak nod. I whispered a quick prayer for him to be alive when I got back, added a blood stop chant and dashed back to the barn.

The men heard the grey horse trot over to rub noses with Arista's horse. I watched them.

Milo asked, "Bamma, I don't see any people. Maybe we hit them and they fell off in the woods. Would the horse come back by itself?"

The other guy, whose name I now knew was Bamma, answered.

"Oh yeah, a horse would do that, but I don't think we hit them both. I think they're sneaking around out there trying not to piss themselves."

Milo laughed. He yanked the third person around so they were facing Bamma.

I recognized Tammy. Her face was streaked with mascara, she'd been crying. I couldn't tell if she was hurt.

Bamma waved the knife at Tammy and spoke, "So, you couldn't tell us where DMac hid his drugs and money. You best start knowing some answers or your usefulness is going to run out. You get me, girlie?"

When Tammy didn't answer Milo gave her a shake. "Yeah, I got it." Her voice was low and submissive. This was not her first rodeo.

Bamma fiddled with the knife. "How many people live here? Where are they and when are they likely to be home?"

Milo shook Tammy again. "Four people live here. Since it's Saturday there's no tellin' where they are or when they'll be home."

A horrible thought hit me. Mom, when was Yvonne bringing her home? I grabbed my phone and sent Yvonne a text. "Keep Mom away from our house tonight. Long story." I prayed she got it. I texted Jana "The guys found our house. Camped out in driveway. Tammy is hostage. Armed." Then a text to Jake. "Baby bro, keep kids away from the house 'til I tell you dif."

Bamma honked the truck horn and yelled, "Hey lady, you got two choices and one of them sucks, for you anyway. You can turn that damn spic over to me and I'll let you and DMac's dumb girlfriend live. If you make me come find you, I will kill both y'all and anyone that happens to come home in the meantime. Oh one more thing. We'll need to relieve you of any money and valuables before we go. I've lost a lot of damn money in this miserable little town. I need something for my trouble."

My phone notified me of incoming messages. I should have silenced it earlier. Fortunately, the alarm is a tiger roar so it's not readily identifiable as a message alert.

"Bamma, what was that noise? It sounded like a growl."

"Hell if I know. Prolly a dog. We're in the boonies. Everyone has a freaking dog in the boonies."

"Didn't sound like no dog. Sounded like something I heard on that Australian animal show." Milo peered towards the woods.

"Stop being paranoid and grow a pair, will ya?" Bamma shook his head at his partner. They flipped each other off.

I read the text replies. Jana's read "10/4 we're coming. Called more backup." A simple thumbs up emoji came from Yvonne. Jacob sent a string of question marks. Then he called. I swiped the decline button and silenced everything. I eased the barn door open and crept inside. I needed to draw them away from Carlos and keep them distracted until the sheriff and his deputies could intervene. If only I could sneak into the house where our guns live.

"Hey lady! That's long enough. Come out and let's chat. Tell me where that big Mexican is, and I'll let you live."

I didn't have a whole lot to work with in the barn. Ian's old muck boots lay in the corner. An idea began to form. I found a couple blankets and set my plan in motion. I scurried over near the opening on the north side of the barn and hollered, "I don't believe you." Then I ran back over by the east end door. I grabbed a shovel and slipped behind some haybales.

Bamma said, "The crazy bitch is in the barn, go check it out. Bring her here."

"What about this girl?"

I heard a slap then Bamma's voice said, "You won't be any trouble, will ya?" A thump and a whimper followed.

I was getting angrier by the minute. *"Keep a cool head baby girl, fear and anger are the enemies of victory." Daddy? Oh my goddess. Daddy's voice hadn't ever been in my head like this. Only Grams.* My eyes began to leak uncontrolled, and my heart beat faster. I was close to collapsing into a puddle. *"None of that now. There's too much at stake."* I took a deep breath and willed my pulse to slow down. I wiped my drippy face on my sleeve. If only snot was a weapon.

I heard the barn door open, and Milo stumbled over the doorsill. He fell over the bale of hay I'd put in the path. He looked up and saw boots sticking out from under a blanket behind some hay. He scrambled over to them and yanked the blanket off. I smacked him in the head with the shovel as hard as I could. If it had been a classic cartoon, we could have seen the stars circle his head as the lights went out. *One down.*

I quickly tied his hands behind his back with a scrap of discarded baling twine. I grabbed my shovel and headed for the door. "Your boy is down, Bamma. Let Tammy go and get out of here while you still can."

I began to chant silently against whatever weapons the redneck moron was apt to pull on me.

I conjure thee, sword or knife, gun or weapon,
By the Spear of Lugh and the Sword of Nuada,
That I am kept from injury as one of the children
Of the Goddess.

(Hexcraft by Silver Raven Wolf 1995)

"Not gonna happen, lady. You seem to think you're callin' the shots here. Milo's an idiot but he is my favorite cousin, so I ain't leaving here without him. He better be alive."

"He's alive for now. I'll trade him for Tammy." A new idea sprang to mind. Not safe and maybe not smart but I had to do something. I texted Jana. Come in silent until you get to the lane. Then hit all the sirens. I may need a distraction. There was no time to wait for a response. Tammy was whimpering louder and pleading for Bamma to stop. I peered out the cracked door. Bamma pinned Tammy against the truck with her arm wrenched in an unnatural position. *Oh God, he's going to cripple her.* I swept through the door and barreled across the parking area.

A siren began to wail close by and I swung my shovel at Bamma's legs. He'd expected me to go high, and he ducked. Tammy used the distraction of my attack to break free and she tore off toward the house. Bamma crumpled to the ground when I buckled his knees. He rolled free and recovered his feet. He limped on one leg. Bamma wheeled to face me and brandished his knife. I swung the shovel at his knife hand, but he switched it to his other hand and dodged back. *An ambidextrous psycho, oh goody.*

He lunged and I blocked. He caught hold of the shovel handle and twisted it. I pulled back then let go. Bamma tumbled backward. I stomped his knee and landed on his chest. He swung the knife at me. I caught his arm with both my hands and rolled away from him. Unfortunately, he rolled with me and was now on top.

I knew I'd made a mistake. All I had left was to pray it wasn't my last mistake. Time slowed down. A memory movie ran through my mind of my children, Michael at our wedding, Michael rescuing me the first time and all the times he taught me Krav Maga.

Bamma tried to switch the knife to his free hand, but I thrashed so hard he'd been using it to keep his balance. Time sped up and a whole bunch of things happened. A small yellow and white streak landed on Bamma's face. Bamma screamed and swatted the kitten away. Hooves pounded across the gravel parking area and BB slid to a stop beside us. I watched my beloved mule grab Bamma's shoulder in his teeth and drag him off of me. He shook him like he was a coyote. *

Yes, dear reader. mules and donkeys will kill coyotes and are often kept with cows, sheep and goats to protect them. Yet another reason they are awesome.

The sheriff, Jana, a third sheriff department vehicle and an ambulance arrived in a storm of dust and gravel. Sophia ran to me and licked my face. She positioned herself between me and Bamma and snarled at him. I'd never seen her so angry.

I closed my eyes and laid my head back. I took some deep breaths. It was over.

"Mew?"

I turned my head to the sound. Bright blue eyes stared at me and a tiny paw smacked me on the nose. "Are you checking to see if I'm alive?"

"Mew!"

I scooped him up. "That was very brave. Not terribly bright. I'm glad you're okay, too." I snuggled the kitten under my chin and stood up. Sheriff Peters told my mule to let the bad man go because he would take it from here. BB stood still and glared at him. Every time Bamma moved ,the mule bit down harder.

Jana rushed up to me and threw her arms around me.

"Omg, Fen, are you alright? I was so worried after you didn't answer my last text. You have to call your brother, he is freaking out." She regained her official deputy demeanor and stepped back.

I walked up to BB and put a hand on his neck. "Hey bubba, good mule. You are so brave. You saved me."

"MEW."

"Right, you and the tiny kitten saved me. Such good boys. I need you to give the bad man to Uncle John. He won't let him hurt us anymore." BB dropped the criminal and backed up.

Lester drove up and rushed up to me.

"Fen, are you okay? I heard the sirens and drove right over. What can I do to help?"

"Thank you for coming. Yes, I'm okay. I've got animals all over the place that need to be secured. Would you take Sophia and the kitten in and bring Tammy outside? Tell her the danger is over. See if she is hurt."

"Can do." Lester scooped Sophia up and held her like a football then he reached for the kitten. Kitty scratched, hissed and puffed up.

"Guess he can stay with me."

Lester nodded and strode toward the house.

Jana wrangled the paramedics and followed me to the barn. They tried to stop at Milo's prone form, but I stopped them. "Nope, he can wait. We have to help Carlos. He was shot and lost a fair amount of blood."

I led them through the barn and out the west side

door to where Carlos lay. He was so still. My eyes burned with fresh tears. I was truly afraid my new friend was dead. New friend, yes, odd as it may seem, the would-be thug that stowed away in my horse trailer three days ago had become my friend.

The EMTs went right to work on Carlos. He was alive. I knew both medics; they were good people and very good at their job. I breathed a sigh of relief and kept silently chanting a healing prayer. They hoisted him onto the gurney, headed for the ambulance in no time.

Jacob and the twins arrived moments after the ambulance left. They were "freaked out to the max," as Arista put it.

After a bazillion assurances that I was fine, I dispatched them to go collect the grey horse who was wandering around in the field with a full set of tack.

A cursory exam of Milo illuded to a concussion. Jana cuffed Milo and read him his rights. She loaded him into a squad car. He'd whined like he was dying.

"Getting smacked in the head with a shovel will do that. Stop being a criminal."

She'd turned her attention to Deputy Sharp. "Take this doofus to the hospital and make sure he's fit to ride a jail cell."

"Sure thing, Captain."

Bamma had been secured by Sheriff Peters in hand cuffs and leg irons. Bamma was short for *Alabama Butcher* and his reputation preceded him. Uncle John took zero chances. Jana would follow the sheriff to the jail. No one would be alone with Bamma.

Tammy was basically unhurt, bruised and scared.

Peters told us to come to the station the next day and

give statements. He wanted to get the perps under lock and key. He'd seen enough with his own eyes to hold them in jail.

I took my mule to the barn and removed his tack. I brushed him down and checked him for injuries. Kitty *helped.* Once BB had his feed, fresh water, and an extra handful of yum yum treats, I hugged him goodnight and went in the house. The twins recovered the grey horse and dealt with his needs. He was uninjured.

I flung myself into a chair at the kitchen island and put my head in my hands. Now I had time to cry but the tears wouldn't come. I felt like a wrung-out dishrag. Lester placed a steaming cup of coffee, complete with his *special sauce* in front of me without a word. I took a sip and savored the burn. "Bless you kind sir."

Tammy sat a few chairs down from me. She fidgeted with a napkin. "Fen, you saved me, again. Thank you. I didn't want to bring them here. That guy made me. He said he'd hurt Brandy if I didn't show them where you live." She burst into tears.

Dammit. I don't have the energy to deal with her angst. I refrained from the temptation to ignore her, run to my bedroom and hibernate. Instead, I turned to Tammy. "Hey, I know they made you. I could see how they treated you. I'm so glad you weren't harmed. At least Brandy wasn't with you. Where is she anyway?"

Arista walked in. "Brandy went skating with us. We dropped her off at her house because we didn't know her mom was a hostage. By the way, she is freaking out because you don't have your phone. Do you want to use mine to call her?" She handed her phone to Tammy.

"Momma, Uncle Jake wants to know if you want

him to go pick up something for dinner."

I thought for a moment. Hibernation wasn't off the table, but it would have to wait. "I want to go to the hospital and check on Carlos. We can drop Tammy off at home on the way to town and hit the Asian buffet before they close."

Arista glanced at Tammy and nodded. "Sounds like a plan, I'll go let Uncle Jake know."

Tammy concluded her call and put Arista's phone on the counter. She'd overheard the plan to get her home and seemed eager to go.

Ten minutes later we were all jammed into my king cab truck. Ian talked Lester into going with us. I asked my brother to drive.

We arrived at the regional hospital with full bellies. The local Asian restaurant did not disappoint. The charge nurse refused to allow all of us to go into see Carlos.

CHAPTER 26

The sheriff left special instructions that paved the way for me to visit him. I hesitated at the door and held my breath as I opened it. The nurse was allowed to let me see him but due to HIPPA rules couldn't explain his condition to me without his consent. Thus far he'd not done any paperwork.

Carlos was awake when I walked in. He smiled when he saw me. The smile was laced with pain and when he spoke his voice was raspy.

"Miss Fen, you are safe. What happened? I woke up here. The last thing I remember is you telling me to be quiet that you were going to face those terrible men. I tried to get up to help but I passed out."

"Hello, my friend. Yes, I am safe, and those guys are in jail. I'm so happy you are alive. I was worried about you. What does the doctor say?"

"He said I was lucky. The bullet went through my right side. It grazed my liver and missed everything else. If it had been even a centimeter to the left or lower, I would have died before they could fix it."

"Wow, but you will make a full recovery?"

"Si. The doctor packed the hole with medicine. He said we must avoid infection, and I must rest. Avoid heavy lifting so the bleeding don't start again."

"Excellent! When you get released from the hospital you can stay with us while you recover if you want to. In the meantime, do you need anything? Can you eat regular food?"

"I would like that, yes. I can eat whatever I want, I think. So far, they just bring me Jello. It's not even red Jello."

"Here's my cell phone number and my brother Jacob's in case I don't answer. You call if you need something. I'll smuggle in a cheeseburger tomorrow.

"Many thanks, Señora. I look forward to hearing the story of you facing down those men."

When I finally fell into bed Saturday night I felt as if every ounce of energy and strength had been wrung out of me. I woke up three and a half hours later than usual the following morning. There was a large cat asleep on my legs and a tiny one on my chest. I studied the kitten. I hadn't taken time to ponder his behavior the last few days. The way he escaped the house and attacked Bamma yesterday was remarkable. He was like a tiny, furry tornado. On the other hand, he'd taken up with Carlos immediately as if he knew he was a decent man, and we were destined to become friends with the big guy. I really needed to figure out a name for the little beastie.

The house was quieter than usual, even for a Sunday. The teenagers were asleep, and Mom wasn't yet home from Yvonne's. Jacob sat by the fireplace with a tablet on his lap. His head lolled to one side. He startled awake when I entered the family room.

"Morning bro', I didn't mean to startle you. Sorry 'bout that. Where's Jana?"

Jacob grinned. "I wasn't scared or asleep. I was resting my eyes. Jana went into the station early to help Peters sort out the charges on those two guys. She told me they planned to lean on that other guy, I forgot his name, to see if he will spill now that the other two are caught. She muttered something about 'he who talks first gets the best deal'."

"Ah, I see. Do they think Donald Gibson is in cahoots with Milo and Bamma somehow?" I'd walked toward the kitchen with coffee in mind. Jacob got up to follow me.

"The possibility was mentioned. They're kicking several theories around. Here, let me get that." Jacob took over the job of making another pot of coffee.

I'd drained the pot and sat down to sip my coffee. "I'm supposed to go in and give my statement today. I'm so far behind on holiday preparations. The past week has been a whirlwind."

Jacob and I chatted about holiday plans, and we agreed to divide the list and conquer it. He's a good brother.

Arista's suspension was over the following day. She shared her mixed feelings about going to school. "It's only one day and then Christmas vacation starts."

Monday evening she told us it had been a "craptastic day full of make-up tests while sequestered in home room." She didn't get to see her friends until sixth period study hall, and they all got in trouble for talking.

I laughed. "Why are y'all talking in class? You spend half the night texting or on the phone with them. Surely you can behave quietly for an hour of study hall."

"Oh Momma, it's not the same. You know that." Arista's smile accompanied her signature eye roll.

Auntie Lou rolled into town on Tuesday evening, and we celebrated Winter Solstice on Wednesday with a bonfire and a feast. Carlos got out of the hospital on Friday and moved into the guest room recently vacated by Tammy.

On Christmas Eve the house filled to the brim for another feast. Jacob and Ian added leaves to the table, and it was still a tight fit. Sheriff Peters, aka Uncle John, came and brought his lovely wife, Celeste. She and Auntie Lou always bond over their mutual love for the city of New Orleans. Brandy came with Tammy and they brought her grandma from Springfield. Zoey, Tom and JJ joined us as well. Jana was on my brother's arm and all dressed up. She looked so pretty in a midnight blue dress under a sheer shawl. I felt like a slob and excused myself to change out of my faded jeans and sweatshirt. I was glad I did because Will Spencer showed up for dinner too and he brought his dog Brutus.

I tried to cover my surprise with a wide smile and warm greeting but missed the mark. I saw Arista whispering to her twin across the room. I knew my conniving daughter invited the handsome vet on my behalf. *Brat.* She saw my expression and winked at me. I saw Ian laugh. *Traitor.*

Will looked very nice in dark brown Dockers and a cream-colored shirt. He saw my expression and his smile faded.

"I'm sorry, Fen, I should have called to make sure it was okay for me to come over. I'm not sure who sent the text invitation, but I suspect it wasn't you."

I grabbed his hand. "No, I'm glad to see you. I'd thought you might go to your parents for the holidays, and it didn't occur to me to invite you here. I'm happy that someone did it for me."

We both stood there blushing like grade schoolers. It was lame. My mom rescued us both when she called out.

"Fen, honey, I think the food is done." I dropped Will's hand like a hot rock and dashed to the kitchen.

After dinner while we were all gathered around the table, Uncle John told Carlos that he'd received the approved form from Immigration.

He took an envelope out of his inside jacket pocket and slid it across the table to the big man. "This is your green card and associated documents. Keep them in a safe place and welcome to the States. Thank you for your help on putting those guys behind bars."

There were cheers from the gathered guests and more than a few glasses clinked together.

Carlos' smile was at least a thousand watts. "I owe many thanks to you, Sheriff, for helping me. It has long been my dream to be here legally. I would not have chosen to witness the crimes or lose my fingers, but this is a Silver Cloud."

I smiled when no one corrected his English. The

faces around my table belonged to wonderful, kind people and my heart swelled with happiness for knowing them.

I wanted to ask Uncle John for a status update on the cases but was reluctant to do so with so many people around. I didn't want to put him on the spot.

It was as if he read my mind. The sheriff tapped on his glass to get our attention.

"While I've got y'all here, I might as well tell you how the investigation has progressed. As most of you know, we had three deaths in the county this month from unnatural causes."

Murmurs rose from the table occupants. Several hadn't heard about the John Doe burned up in the RV. I glanced at Uncle John and shushed the crowd. "There was a fire in an RV last week. A search revealed a body inside. The second death was Darren McNamara who was found dead downtown behind the gym." I left out the grisly part about him being impaled on a bale spike since we'd all just eaten. I need not have bothered.

"Was that the guy that was skewered on the antique bale spike?" asked Tom. He licked the last bit of whip cream from his fork.

Poor Yvonne paled, but my mother didn't bat an eye. *Nothing much bothers her, probably the steady diet of NCIS crime drama built up her resistance.*

"Yep Tom, that was him." Ian elbowed his buddy and gave a slight motion toward the older ladies.

Tom blushed and mumbled something that sounded like "sorry."

I picked up the story from there. "Then I found the body of a gentleman over at the city park, he'd been shot."

Carlos shook his head. "My apologies to the dead but Eddie G., he was no gentleman."

Uncle John cleared his throat and attention returned to him. "As I was about to say, two of the three deaths were ruled as homicides. Donald Gibson killed Darren McNamara behind the gym. He hit him with a baseball bat that we believe he'd taken away from the victim."

Brandy nodded and said, "I remember leaving my bat in his truck when he picked me up from school."

The sheriff nodded. "Mr. Gibson claims that Darren brandished the bat at him, and they fought. He denies drugs being involved and blames his anger on the fact that Darren beat Gibson's dog to near death. So, he hit McNamara and tossed him on the spike in a fit of rage."

Dr. Spencer spoke up. "I treated that dog. He was in bad shape and the owner, Mr. Gibson, was very upset. I remember when he brought the dog back for a follow up. He looked as if he'd been in a fight, though he told me it was a car accident. The man hadn't had a scratch on him the first time he was in with his dog. Fen, do you remember? I think you were in my office both times."

"I do remember that." I'd taken a bite of cake and covered my mouth with my napkin.

Uncle John gestured with three fingers, glanced at Carlos and retracted his hand. "The third guy was a Hispanic man called Eddie G. He was shot by Bamma, and Milo was an accomplice to that murder. Neither he nor Milo are talking at all. All the suspects deny involvement in the death of the guy in the RV. Although Donald Gibson alleges that Darren McNamara stole drugs from the RV location and McNamara was the registered owner of the RV. Our efforts to substantiate those allegations have not been fruitful." He glanced down the table at Tammy.

Tammy shrugged. "I didn't even know Darren owned an RV. He never told me, and we sure never went camping or anything fun."

Peters shook his head. "The fire marshal concluded the fire was of *undetermined cause* and the medical examiner has yet to figure out why the person died. Or if they were already dead when the fire started. We may never know exactly what happened out there."

After the dishes were cleared everyone broke up into groups to chat or play games.

Yvonne and Mom challenged Jacob and Jana to a card game known as Pitch. Uncle John asked Will about Brutus's police training. It sounded like he was hatching a plan to borrow the dog for local departmental business. The big German Shepherd may have flunked police dog school for not being aggressive enough, but he certainly showed up when the time came to take down a real bad guy.

Auntie Lou and I walked through the family room. The television was still on. I recognized the show that played as *Leverage*. What caught my attention was the song. I'd heard that song a few days ago. The kitten hopped up in front of the TV and pawed at the screen. When the chorus came on, "That's just me thinking of you..." Kitty launched himself at me and clung to my leg. I heard a word in my head and locked eyes with the little beast. "Kane. Your name is Kane."

"Mew!"

EPILOGUE

On Christmas Day the number of people in the house was back to normal. Carlos was the only extra one. He chatted on a video call with his mother and siblings. I heard him tell them he liked it here and would be staying a while.

Later in the day my college roommate called with news. She'd been on the road doing mobile photography for a few years. Then several months ago her beloved great uncle had passed and left her his bar. I'd never been there but the description put me in mind of a cross between the bar in Cheers and the bar in Roadhouse. Homey, country, a bet dingy but everyone knows your name. She went on to tell me, since she took over the bar there were several misadventures. Turned out the bar was haunted. I heard a crash in the background, and she had to go. Darcy promised to tell me more very soon.

ABOUT THE AUTHOR

Jen Kenning was born in Iowa and has called Southwest Missouri home for "the important part of her entire life." She always loved hearing and reading stories growing up. Her love of stories slowly morphed into a desire to spin her stories.

Jen has been a maid, waitress, cook, horseback riding trail guide, insurance adjuster, fire and theft investigator, customer service technician, and a reference librarian, among other things. Her favorite jobs were trail guide and librarian.

She currently lives on a family farm with her son and too many pets. When she's not writing she grows microgreens or makes jewelry.

A NOTE FROM JEN:

Dear Reader, I deeply appreciate your time, and I hope you've enjoyed this book. There are more adventures for Fen, her family and friends in the future. You're invited to stay up to date with us on my website: JenKenningAuthor.com. You'll find a few recipes, the odd short story or article and there's even a newsletter to subscribe to. No pressure. 😊

Be Well!
Jen